In sparkling, clear prose, understated yet unflinching, *Open Season* probes deep into the fissures of caste, class, religion, and gender in our world. With references that range from the classical poets Ghalib, Meer, and Rumi to Hardy Boys, Dickens, and Shakespeare, *Open Season*, like many Canadian diasporic writings, expands the boundaries of Canadian literature, tearing down the high fences to let the new realities of the globalized world in.

ARUN PRABHA MUKHERJEE,
Professor Emerita, York University

Intensely atmospheric, Shaukat Ajmeri's stories transport you easily to times and places. You hear the voice of each character speaking, while the words evoke the setting in your mind. These are stories that take us to places which might otherwise be inaccessible.

TEHMINA KHAN,
author of *Things She Could Never Have*

"The day my school principal caned me, because my hair was not cut short enough, my grandmother died." The moment you read this sentence you know that you are in the company of a genuine fiction writer. The stories of Shaukat Ajmeri are endearing in their simplicity, and for their love of life and people. They make you aware that it is our relationships which give us our humanity.

APOORVANAND,
Professor, Hindi Department, University of Delhi

Open Season secures Ajmeri's importance in the firmament of diaspora writing, as a straightforward but powerful storyteller, who has inherited O Henry's love for the telling twist, but who situates his narratives in multitudes of contexts and perspectives befitting the complexity of his motherland.

KIRAN BHAT,
author of *We of the Forsaken World*

OPEN SEASON

STORIES

SHAUKAT AJMERI

MAWENZI
HOUSE

We acknowledge the support of the Canada Council for the Arts for our publishing program. We also acknowledge support from the Government of Ontario through the Ontario Arts Council, and the support of the Government of Canada through the Canada Book Fund.

Canada Council for the Arts Conseil des arts du Canada

ONTARIO ARTS COUNCIL
CONSEIL DES ARTS DE L'ONTARIO
an Ontario government agency
un organisme du gouvernement de l'Ontario

Canada

Cover design by Kaamil Ajmeri
Cover photo: anandnagori / Rajasthani Door stock photo / iStockphoto.com

Library and Archives Canada Cataloguing in Publication

Title: Open season : stories / Shaukat Ajmeri.

Names: Ajmeri, Shaukat, 1961- author.

Identifiers: Canadiana (print) 20240344847 | Canadiana (ebook) 20240344863 | ISBN 9781774151556 (softcover) | ISBN 9781774151563 (EPUB) | ISBN 9781774151570 (PDF)

Subjects: LCGFT: Short stories.

Classification: LCC PS8601.J64 O64 2024 | DDC C813/.6—dc23

Printed and bound in Canada by Coach House Printing

Mawenzi House Publishers Ltd.
39 Woburn Avenue (B)
Toronto, Ontario M5M 1K5
Canada

www.mawenzihouse.com

People tire themselves out building a house
And you feel no pity in burning down neighbourhoods

BASHIR BADR

I'm thinking—
Today, all these
Thoughts inside my mind
That I'm writing down on paper
It's only for those who
Can leave life's traditions
And difficulties
And griefs
Outside the door,
And have the courage
To live
The truth of their minds.

AMRITA PRITAM

CONTENTS

Acknowledgements

I want to thank my friend Anil Menon for being the first victim on whom these stories were inflicted. He was gracious in his criticism and ruthless in his edits. I'm grateful to Urbi Bhaduri for her insightful comments and for helping me refine and reshape the initial draft. I owe immense gratitude to MG Vassanji for constantly demanding "where is the story", and thus compelling me to revisit some of the tales in search of that elusive beast. His edict to me was: "put some pith in your stories, a punch; be suspicious of your characters, even if they are like your mother and father." This became my guiding light as I reworked and revised the stories, and I hope fellow writers would take this excellent advice to inform their labours and profit from it. I must thank Nurjehan Aziz for her meticulous, fine-combed reading of the final draft, and if errors still persist the culpability will entirely be mine. I must also express my gratitude to Sabrina Pignataro for her eye for detail and for designing and putting together this book.

I want to thank my sons, Danish and Kaamil for their love and support, and my wife, Shahnaz for putting up with my long absences and for letting me spend an insane amount of time on this indulgence—a privilege which I cherish with humility and gratitude. Lastly, none of this would be possible without my muse, the little fairy who sits on my shoulder and whispers in my ear "write, write." Ghalib has said it the best:

Words come to mind from the unknown and unseen,
Ghalib, the pen's scratching is but an angel's whisper

The Reading Ritual

1

I stood at the gate of our house and looked on wistfully as my sister Neha left to go out with her friends. She didn't take me with her because I was not old enough—or rather, good enough. I was thirteen—she was fifteen—and at that point in our lives, we measured our age differences by weeks and months, if not days. I couldn't wait to grow up, but the thought kept nagging me that no matter how old I grew, I would always remain younger, forever condemned to be the baby sister. There would always be this insurmountable hump. The injustice of it all!

Neha had gone out only a few paces when she turned and strode back toward me.

"Will you be home when I return?" she whispered.

"I don't know. If Ma goes out, I'll go with her. Why?"

"Nothing."

"Tell me!"

"Because I don't want to be alone."

Was she saying what I thought she was saying? I was not the

only one then. Neha was not only older but also smarter, and here she was, as afraid to be home alone as I was. Just as I opened my mouth to say something, she turned and left. The moment passed.

Our large joint family of aunts, uncles, cousins, and grandparents lived in a two-storey house on a quiet tree-lined street. Sunday mornings presented a beehive of activity. Men were off from work, the children off from school, and the women as usual—or more than usual—busy in the kitchen, ministering to the men, or attending to us kids and our shenanigans. The women never had a day off. Mother used to complain about it, to which Father would retort, "What do you *do* all day, anyway?" And she would get mad. "We slave all day long," she would say, "and even at night can't sleep before performing our duty." I always wondered what that duty might be.

We had a large courtyard in the middle of the house. Paved with slate flagstone, it was open to the sky, and we children spent a lot of our free time here, playing, chatting and generally horsing around. Neha and I would join our boy cousins in their games. Rakesh taught me how to hold a cricket bat and how to swing my arm when bowling. But we girls could never get the hang of it. We could not muster the masculine poise—the easy confidence that came so naturally to them. We could never hold the bat at the correct angle. I would stand at the crease with my legs stiff, heels close together, torso straight like a bamboo stalk. The bat would be flat outward, and I could never manage to tap it on the ground with the swagger that Rakesh showed. When I swung at the ball, Ramesh, my other cousin, would say, "You are holding a bat, not a broom." And everyone would laugh.

When I was bowled out—one could never be sure of the decision, because the stumps were drawn on the wall with charcoal—I would challenge the decision and refuse to budge. This would be followed by a shouting match, Ramesh calling me a bad loser and a crybaby. He would then declare loudly that they would not play with girls anymore. But to make up the numbers, they had to come back begging to us.

Apart from our textbooks, we had no inclination to read. The only thing widely read in our home was the newspaper. On Sunday mornings, Father and our uncles took turns to read the paper, thus avoiding a mad scramble. Among the women, Sushma Auntie, Ramesh's mother, read a women's magazine called *Sarita*. She had a pile of them in her room. Our mother never encouraged us to read anything other than textbooks.

"Life is the best teacher," she would say, sneering at Sushma Auntie's reading habit. "Books only confuse the mind—fill you up with ideas and knowledge for which you have no use."

All this changed when Sharda Devi came to live next door. It was a large estate with sprawling lawns dotted with stately neem, jacaranda, and gulmohar trees. High walls fenced off the property from prying eyes. As far as I could remember, no one had lived there for the longest time. The wrought-iron gate had always been padlocked, and the driveway overgrown with grass and bramble. Then one day I saw the gate open. The driveway had been cleaned up and a car was parked at the end of it. The hedges had been trimmed and the outer walls sparkled with a fresh coat of bright white lime paint. As for the house proper, we could barely see it from the road.

One Sunday afternoon, when I was playing outside our home, a car stopped and a woman in a dark blue sari with a shiny pink border and sporting a large red bindi on her forehead called out and asked my name.

"Oh, Priya is a really nice name," she said. "I'm your neighbour. You should come over, I've got something for you."

I nodded, not sure what to make of it. When I told my mother, she was suspicious at first and said that maybe the woman had some ulterior motive. But then her curiosity got the better of her. She asked me what this woman looked like. I said she looked nice and well dressed. Then she asked me how old she was.

"How do I know how old people are?" I protested. "Like you!"

Then she asked who else was in the car, and I reported that she had been sitting alone at the back, and a uniformed chauffeur was at the wheel.

"Rich party," said Father from his desk where he was working on the day's accounts. "They own lands up north and the family lives in America. Maybe they have moved back."

Mother's interest was piqued; she said I could go visit Sharda Devi but warned me never to go alone. "You and Neha. Always go together."

The following Sunday, after finishing our homework, we decided to visit Sharda Devi. As we walked up the driveway, placing our feet in the fresh car tracks, a servant emerged from the outhouse. He had probably heard us opening the gate. We said we wanted to meet auntie. He asked us to sit, pointing to the chairs on the veranda, and went inside.

The house was of stone brick, and of colonial vintage, as I now realize. Flower beds surrounded the house. The doors and windows had received fresh paint, of which a faint scent hung in the air. The front lawn had a short hedge and was sprouting new grass. A black rubber hose sprinkled water upon the greenery. Neha and I sat quietly, a little nervous with anticipation.

"I would feel scared to be here at night," Neha said. I nodded in agreement.

The servant, whom we would soon learn to call Ramu Kaka, said that madam would be with us soon. He asked if we wanted anything to eat or drink. We shook our heads.

In a little while, Sharda Devi joined us.

"Priya, right?" she exclaimed. "I'm so glad you came. And who is this, your sister?"

I introduced Neha, and she said we were as pretty as our names.

In those days, whenever we met new people, we were subjected to a full interrogation—about our school, our favourite subjects, our hobbies, our friends. Our enthusiasm in responding depended on whether we liked the person or not. Sharda Devi asked none of those questions. To our young eyes, she looked regal and had a certain polish in her manner and speech that we had not seen in any other aunties we knew. There was something magnetic about her.

She insisted we eat something and asked Ramu Kaka to bring sweets and lemonade. We hadn't heard the word "lemonade" before, but surmised that it might have to do with lemons—maybe it was nimbu paani? Neha and I looked at each other and smiled. My mouth watered and my mind kept harping on the word. It sounded so foreign and classy that the humble nimbu paani acquired new respect in my eyes. It even tasted better when I drank it.

Unlike other hosts, who normally sat back and watched their guests eat, Sharda Devi joined us in partaking of the snacks. She even commented that the lemonade was good and refreshing, to which we nodded vigorously, smacking our lips. She asked us whether we read books and was visibly dismayed at our answer. After we finished eating, she led us into the house. It was dark and faintly musty inside. The windows were large and many and were flung open. A breeze played with the chintz curtains. The semicircular transoms above the windows were studded with stained glass, refracting the outside light in muted colours. It felt quiet and eerie and—for an instant—Mother's warning of "Don't go there alone" crossed my mind.

But I didn't feel threatened in any way. Sharda Devi was

cool and the house had a museum-like charm about it, albeit a museum badly organized. Things were all over the place. Sharda Devi apologized for the mess. "Too much stuff to take care of. I'm arranging and putting away things slowly. Deciding what to put where is not easy, you know."

We picked our way through multitudes of boxes and crates and stopped at a room that looked as if books had rained there. I instinctively looked up at the ceiling. Sharda Devi cleared a space on the floor and we all sat down. She looked around and grabbed a large bound book. "This is an atlas," she said and opened it.

The only map I had ever seen was the one that hung on the back wall of our classroom, to which nobody ever paid any attention. This was different. As Sharda Devi turned the coloured pages, pointing at the different continents and countries, I became curious. She turned to a map of India and showed us Delhi, Bombay, Madras, and Calcutta, cities we had heard about. Then she came to Rajasthan.

"This is our state," she said. She turned to a larger map of Rajasthan and put her finger on Udaipur, saying, "This is our city." Sitting in Udaipur, I was looking at Udaipur on a map. It felt as if I was inside and outside the city at the same time. I found this intriguing. Then Sharda Devi asked, "Do you hear anything in here?"

I perked up my ears and listened intently. Apart from the ambient sounds of an inhabited place, there was nothing. Neha and I shook our heads.

"Try again, listen carefully."

We again shook our heads.

"Can't you hear the cries of the stories trapped inside these books?" she asked and swept her hand around the room. "If you could hear the words speak—as I can—you would know that the only thing they desire is that somebody read them. Think of words as animals and birds. When writers write them down, words become trapped, caged as if they were in a zoo. The only way to free them is by reading them. That is their only salvation. Words want to be read, they long to be rescued by us. I buy books because I love words and the stories they tell, and by reading them I set them free."

I stared at her, mesmerized.

"Isn't it strange that words give voice to our thoughts but themselves are voiceless?"

What was she talking about? I was puzzled.

Seeing the bafflement on our faces, Sharda Devi smiled. "My dears, don't look so confused, I'm not mad." She rummaged through a pile of books close at hand and picked a small bound volume. She showed us the cover: *Shakuntala*. "Have you heard the story of Shakuntala?" she asked. "No? Okay, let me read it to you, and you will know what I mean. It's in Hindi."

She started reading the story in her soft voice, pausing now and then for effect and to see the expressions on our faces. I could feel the delight in her voice; as she pronounced the words, it seemed that she was actually setting them free, and this generated a tremor of enchantment in me. She read two other stories, this time in English, whose names I cannot recall.

By the time she finished, it was past afternoon. How quickly time had passed. We said it was lunch time and Mother would be waiting. She said she wanted to give us books to read. Knowing Mother's aversion to them, Neha declined politely.

"We'll come again and you can read to us," she said.

Sharda Devi smiled, "That I'd love to, but you must do your part as well. Remember, you have to liberate the words."

We nodded and took a couple of books. We would have to explain to Mother somehow.

The visits to Sharda Devi's became regular, two or three times a week. Most days, Neha and I went together, but there were times when I went alone—when Neha had homework or was going out with friends. Mother pried every little detail out of us about our neighbour's house and life. About Sharda Devi herself, we gave a glowing account. Though initially jealous, our mother gradually and grudgingly accepted that the lady had a certain charm and class that she herself could only aspire to. She was happy that we could learn a few smart things from her, that her sophistication would rub off on us. She no longer minded my going alone.

Mother changed her opinion about books too, when we told her about Sharda Devi's love of stories and about her passion to liberate words. So much so, she also started reading, and borrowed magazines from Sushma Auntie. We teased her. "Ma, don't read, it's going to mess up your mind!" And she would retort by taking a dig at our mentor, "Well, I have to do my part in freeing the words."

Ramu Kaka had three children, two boys and a girl, all older than us. Sharda Devi made sure that they went to a local government school. The girl, Leela, who was around eighteen years old, was hired to work at our house in the evenings. She did the dishes and cleaned up the kitchen after the women had finished cooking. On Sundays, she would come in the morning and dust and sweep the entire house. Her brothers, Mohan and Mangesh, were twins, a year younger than her. Mangesh walked with a limp, one foot having been deformed by polio. Their mother had died of jaundice when they were in their early teens.

The twins would come to our house and do odd jobs for us. Grandfather gave them a small stipend. Sometimes they joined us in games, and when it was time for cricket, our cousins started telling Neha and me to scoot off, because Mohan and Mangesh made up the requisite number. The three servant kids were a godsend for our family. Everyone sang praises of Sharda Devi and her willingness to share her helpers with her neighbours.

I now find it strange that Sharda Devi never invited us, or why we did not invite her over. Maybe her refinement and wealth made us feel inadequate. Sharda Devi herself also showed little interest in meeting our parents. She never ever asked about them, though in our own childish way we volunteered information about our household, telling her almost everything that happened at home. She was highly amused when we told her about Mother's newfound love of books. To her credit, she never asked follow-up questions or evinced any inquisitiveness. Nor did she ever tell us anything about herself. We knew that she was married, because she wore a mangalsutra around her neck and streaked the parting of her hair with vermilion. Then why did she live alone? Why had she relocated from America? Did she have any children? Where was her husband?

As the weeks went by, the clutter around her house began to clear and things began to find their places. One of the walls in the main hall got covered with photographs, arranged in a strangely striking pattern. In the middle of the arrangement was a large photo showing four women's faces. They were all laughing and one of them was Sharda Devi.

In the library, or the reading room, the books were now arranged on shelves in glass cupboards along the walls. In the centre of the room, on a faded Persian rug, there was a couch facing the windows, with a coffee table in front of it. On a writing desk set in a corner of the room was a family photograph. Sharda Devi looked much younger in it. A man, tall and dapper, dressed in a suit and tie, stood beside her with an arm around her shoulders. Two small girls, with short hair and ribbons sticking out, stood in front of them.

One day she read us a story about two children who were lost in a forest. Their mother was inconsolable and could not stop crying. Midway through the story, Sharda Devi closed the book and said, wearily, "We will finish it some other time." Her voice sounded as though coming from a great distance. I sensed her sadness.

"Where is your family, Auntie ji?"

Sharda Devi took a breath. Tears brimmed her eyes. She reached out, took my hands in hers, and hugged me. "I'll tell you some other time," she said and told me to hurry along as it was getting late. I said goodbye and left.

At the gate, Mohan was chatting with his friends. On seeing me, they fell quiet. I threw a quick glance at them and kept walking. A moment later he called out to me.

I stopped and turned around. He was a skinny lad, dark and lanky. There was nothing about him that made you want to look at him or talk to him. His mullet hairstyle was an eyesore. He fussed over his hair obsessively, with a small comb he kept on the ready. Pocketing his comb now and smoothing his hair, he smiled, baring his yellow teeth.

"What?" I asked in a gruff tone. Even at that age I was conscious of his status as a servant.

He hesitated, looked around shiftily, then said, "Would you read stories to me?"

"What?"

"Sharda Devi reads stories to you. You can read them to me."

"You can read, do it yourself," I said dismissively.

"But you enjoy them more if somebody reads to you."

I shrugged and walked away. The idea of reading to him unsettled me. It suggested an exercise in intimacy. You just couldn't read to any random person. Mohan was older, a servant, a boy; he had no business being in the same space as I was.

But I had little idea of his determination.

2

One afternoon, Mohan came into my room. I was doing my homework and looked up in surprise. He came up straight to my desk and asked what I was doing.

"Can't you see I'm doing my homework?"

"Oh. I was wondering if you would read a story to me."

"I'm busy."

"I'll wait."

I did not respond. He sat down on the floor near the door and stared at me. I continued doing my work. When I finished, I said I couldn't oblige him. He insisted and begged. Since I was going to read anyway, I relented and told him that I would read to him this one time only. He agreed, and I began reading. But he said that he could not hear me clearly and tapped the floor at his side. Without thinking, I went and sat beside him, keeping my distance. He got up and shut the door, and when he sat back down, I noticed that he had moved in closer.

"We don't want to disturb others," he said.

I read a couple of stories by Shivani, and he listened with rapt attention. Once, when I turned to look at him, I found his eyes upon me. I felt a twinge of discomfort, but he said he loved the way I read, and would like to come again if I did not mind. I said nothing, but my initial resistance was melting away.

"Let this be our little game," he said and left.

Days passed. Whenever he came around to run errands and play cricket, he did not so much as look at me. I did find this attitude strange. Was *this* the little game he was alluding to?

Yet every other week or so, he would sneak into my room, and I would wonder how he knew I would be alone. It never occurred to me to ask. We hardly ever talked. He would sit by the door and wait till I finished my homework. All that time, he would stare at me, and I began to feel uneasy. But his good behaviour was reassuring. And he was a servant after all, he must know his place and limits. I never imagined that he could hurt me in any way.

One afternoon we were sitting next to each other, propped by cushions against the wall, our legs stretched out. As I read, he suddenly put his hand on my thigh over my dress. I stopped midsentence.

"I like your frock," he said and started feeling the material with his fingers.

I kept reading. He held the hem for a while, and then let go, and in doing so, moved it up a little and let his hand fall on my bare thigh. I was petrified. "Keep reading," he said, in a tone that I found mildly threatening. I continued reading haltingly, my heart beating fast, my throat dry. His hand stayed in place on my thigh, motionless. His touch burnt my skin, and I almost felt that it would come off when he removed his hand. I finished the story somehow, and closed the book. He asked me to read more but I said I was tired. He got up and left, but not before reminding me that this was our little game—that if anybody came to know, we both would be in trouble.

I was scared and knew that something bad had happened that day. I reasoned that the transgression would not happen again, I would not *allow* it to happen again. But I could not prevent the times when I was alone, and unfailingly Mohan visited me at those times. He would tell me to do my homework later and read to him first. I obeyed, and with every visit, his hands progressed up my thigh, inch by inch. I would stop reading and close my eyes. He would force his hand between my legs, pry them apart and caress the skin on the inner side. One day he reached right up between my legs.

I was stiff with fear. I wanted to shove his hand away, but could not bring myself to do it. My hands had suddenly lost their power, it was as if my mind and body were two separate things, the first having no control over the second. Then on another occasion, he took my hand and placed it on his pants and rubbed his thing with it. I was like a dummy, a puppet ceding all control to my manipulator. I closed my eyes, as if to deny what was happening, as if by not seeing it I could make it go away.

His visits became more and more frequent, and every time I felt frightened and helpless like a caged bird. The pretence of reading had been discarded, and "the little game" had fallen into a routine. We would sit side by side, his hand would reach between my thighs, and he would take my hand to massage his crotch. I would let him do it, my eyes closed in denial, waiting for him to have his fill and leave.

This continued for more than six months. Some nights I would wake up in terror, my body pouring sweat. At school I was listless and fell behind in my studies. I dreaded being alone. I was scared to talk about it to anyone. It would only invite trouble, as Mohan had said, and I just did not have the words to describe what was happening. I had a sense of being violated, I knew that it was bad, and wrong, but my young mind was not able to grasp the enormity of it. All the stories I had read—of brave heroes surmounting great odds—had failed to equip me with the courage to say no, to make a noise, to get up and leave.

I began to avoid him. When he was in the house doing errands, or playing with our cousins, I would retire to my room. I stopped going to Sharda Devi's; I dreaded seeing him there. My sister had not taken to reading as much as I had, nor had she been as enthralled by Sharda Devi, so she never asked me why I had stopped going there. But Mother did, and I told her that between school and studies and friends, there wasn't much time left for Sharda Devi. Besides, I could read on my own. I don't think she ever bought that, though.

Sharda Devi too, it seemed, never missed us. Her silence was a sort of repudiation, a rejection that bothered me. Knowing her reserved and incurious nature, I doubted she would ever ask Leela about us, yet I continued to hope that she might send a message at least, asking why we had stopped visiting her. I came to associate reading with what Mohan was doing to me. It had all started with books, and I naively thought that it might all end if I stopped reading. Who knew that the pursuit of liberating words could lead to my own bondage?

One April evening, Mohan came and said that it was his birthday and I must give him a present. He took my hand into his pants, pleasured himself and then squirted his stuff on it. I was horrified. I ran blindly to the bathroom and washed my hands manically, fearing that the stuff might leave a stain. I glanced at the mirror and noticed that I was crying. At that moment I swore, come what may, I would never, ever be alone in my room. I insisted on going out with Mother or Neha, and when, for some reason I could not, I would go to Sushma Auntie's or our grandmother's room.

As I think back to those days, I cannot understand why I had never thought of doing that before. I cannot imagine how the guy had the nerve to attempt what he did, and from what I understood of Neha's fear of being left alone, it seemed that I was not his only victim. His audacity was not just astounding in itself but also very reckless, considering the incredible risk he was running. My father was known for his temper, and if he even had an inkling of what Mohan was up to, he would have skinned him alive. Ironically, Father's anger was also one of the reasons that prevented me from speaking.

For several weeks I didn't give Mohan a chance to find me alone. I made sure not to cross his path. On occasion, if I accidentally ran into him and our eyes met, he would glower at me. I paid him no heed; as long as others were around, I had nothing to fear. But one afternoon I was going up the stairs and he was hiding where the stairs turned. He snared me on the landing. Everyone was in their rooms; summer heat and a siesta-induced silence enveloped the house. My heart stopped. If a cheetah smiled on catching a gazelle, that would have resembled the expression he had on his face. His thin frame, the awful mullet, his scraggy, pubescent facial hair and his pathetic attempt at fashion made him look like an evil joker. The very sight of him filled me with revulsion, but at the same time I was scared stiff. He said nothing; he just came on to me as I retreated into a corner, placed his hand on my chest and began pawing me. I closed my eyes. When I could bear it no more, I ducked and ran up the stairs.

Thereafter, waylaying me on the staircase landing became his modus operandi. Ours was an old house; the narrow stone stairs turned at a hairpin at midpoint, and from the landing, one could hear people come up or down before you actually saw them. Mohan, as always, had an uncanny sense of timing. He knew the movements of everyone in the household; he knew the quiet periods, usually the somnolent afternoons and the lull after supper. In the evenings, I barely went out except on an errand for Mother, or on the rare occasion when I was late in returning from a friend's.

Every time I submitted to his groping, my eyes closed and my body turned cold as if dead. It never lasted for more than a few seconds. It would eventually begin to hurt and I would wriggle in discomfort, shake him off, and squeeze my way out. He never held on to me, pushed or forced me to stay put. Perhaps he knew that he couldn't take a chance there, exposed on the stairs. He seemed to be in no hurry, showed no signs of desperation. He had succeeded in keeping me silent, and on that account, assumed that he had nothing to fear. The staircase snare continued for weeks.

One winter evening, a time when darkness arrived early, the streets were quiet and I was returning from Grandma's house with a bowl of kheer. I was almost sprinting, my mind set on getting home, grabbing a spoon and eating the coveted pudding. For some reason, the staircase light was not working. I flipped the switch up and down several times, but to no avail. I started up the stairs, slowly finding the steps with my feet, clutching the bowl in my left hand and feeling the wall with my right.

It was pitch dark. I couldn't see a thing. The sweet anticipation of the kheer was momentarily forgotten as I thought of the trap. The primal fear of darkness combined with the ever-present danger of the predator made me stop. I stood there for a long moment, wanting to turn back. But I reasoned, he has never been here this late. I began groping my way up. As I reached the landing, I heard the sound of human breath; and before I even had the time to feel afraid, two hands grabbed me. A bone-rattling shriek. The bowl flew into his face as though it had suddenly grown wings. A groan, a curse. Then it fell, a loud shattering, the pudding splattering. I cowered into the corner; my arms upright in front of my face like a shield. Kheer dripping from my hands, splotching my clothes. Feeling yucky and terrified I stood there breathless, not understanding what had just happened. A shadow ran down the stairs, and then there was a sound of stumbling and falling. Another curse and a soft howl. Father on hearing the scream had come out. When he asked me what had happened, I said it was a cat.

The kheer, of course, was written off, but the upshot of the incident was that I never saw Mohan again. He disappeared. Possibly he thought I had told on him. His brother, Mangesh, continued coming to the house and did the usual chores. When Grandfather inquired about Mohan, Mangesh said that his brother had gone to Bombay to look for a job. On hearing this, a relief radiated from my soul. My days and my nights would no longer be haunted by that feeling of dread. When I told Neha about it, she let out a deep sigh, as I had expected. We both understood what it meant, but we never talked about it. It was our secret, our secret shame.

Years passed before I took to books again, and with time, the bad memories associated with them began to fade. In fact, when I was in tenth standard, I began reading precisely to erase that past. I missed Sharda Devi, and even though Mohan by all accounts had gone, I just could not bring myself to visit her. I longed to hear her voice again, its gentle cadence; the way she looked up from the pages to smile at me, the way she said my name. I had known her only for a short while, but she had made a big impression on me. Though she revelled in storytelling, she never could tell the story of that family photograph.

3

After I finished my schooling, my life followed the usual trajectory: there was college and then marriage, which brought me to Canada. I visit home every few years. During my last trip, two years ago, I saw Mangesh passing by our house once. I would not have recognized him but for his limp. He looked old beyond his years. Our eyes met, and he too must have recognized me, but a hesitation fostered by twenty intervening years kept us from acknowledging each other. Seeing him brought back the memories. It seemed such a long time ago. But somehow the trauma has lived inside me like a slow fire. It flares up at times, catching me unawares and I can almost feel my skin burning where the lecher had touched me. Over the years, though, I've tried to forget and internalize the anguish, blaming myself for the abuse. Why was I so weak, so powerless? Why did I allow it to happen? In my mind I have relived the scenes a million times, imagining myself standing up to him, walking away, slapping him, doing something to stop him. And a million times I have reasoned and rationalized why I couldn't do it, but nothing satisfies me. On seeing Mangesh that day I suddenly felt anxious. I wanted to breathe, to open my heart, release the trauma to the four winds, as it were. And although Sharda Devi had nothing to do with it, I felt an urge to tell her. She should know, I reasoned unreasonably. Perhaps sharing the pain would ease my burden. I wondered whether she was still alive.

I walked toward her house. The iron gate was rusting, its black paint peeling. The driveway was still unpaved, with deeper ruts now; the gravel on it had been pulverized into dust. But the shrubs and creepers along the boundary wall were thriving, while the bougainvilleas were wild and in full bloom. The lawn in front was also in good repair; Mangesh must be taking good care of it. The house with its chiselled stones still looked solid, though somewhat smaller from what I remembered. The mortar was crumbling in places, and a layer of timeless dust seemed to have settled on the façade, which even the rains had failed to wash away.

I walked around the house to reacquaint myself with the place, to recalibrate the landscape to my memory. All the windows were closed except for the one where the library used to be. The flower beds around the house were thriving with rose bushes, dahlias, lilies, and various kinds of herbs, including a profusion of mint and coriander. The trees, like everything else, had aged but were in no mood to retire; their sylvan canopy nurtured a sense of deep calm. The old feeling of the estate being a park returned, and for a moment I was transported to my thirteen-year-old self who had come here full of anticipation and been overwhelmed by the occasion and the manse. Who could have then imagined what magical vistas would be opened to me, and what unimaginable horrors spawned? In quick succession, a thrill and a shudder traversed my body.

Every sign on the estate suggested that Sharda Devi was still living here. And the presence of a newer model of Maruti in the driveway—the old Fiat must have been retired a long time ago—suggested that she went out and about, too.

I walked up to the front door and rang the bell. I did not hear any stirring inside. Maybe she was asleep, but at this time in the morning? I waited for a few minutes and pressed the button again. No response. I pushed the door a little and it yielded. I opened it slowly and peeked inside—not a soul. With cautious steps and eager eyes, I entered and walked toward the library. Not much had changed. The photograph of the four smiling faces in the hallway caught my eye. Somehow I found it reassuring.

I stopped at the doorway of the library. She was sitting in a wheelchair facing the window. The curtains were drawn open and morning light poured in. From her posture and the way her head was tilted forward, it seemed like she was reading a book, just the way I had expected to see her.

I knocked on the door, and she slowly turned her head.

"Who is it?" she asked, clearing her throat.

I went in and took my seat on a chair beside her. She did not have a book. She might have nodded off, and I had woken her up. She had a faraway look in her eyes. It seemed as though she had been left behind and forgotten. I felt a surge of pity and reached for her hands. They were soft and wrinkled, the skin mottled and thin as parchment, with tributaries of greenish veins under it. I pressed them gently and said, "Sharda Auntie, you remember me?"

She put on the glasses dangling from a string around her neck. Her face had gathered wrinkles, but the ravages of time had failed to completely overrun her innate beauty. She tried to smile as she looked at me, and her whole face seemed to crackle, as if her muscles, having fallen into disuse, couldn't quite conjure it up. But when she finally did, a shadow seemed to lift.

"Oh, Kavita, my sweetheart, I've been waiting for you," she said, and then looking behind me, asked, "Where is Kaveri, your sister? She didn't come with you?"

I was puzzled, not sure whom she was referring to. Perhaps her two daughters, and I glanced at the family photograph on the table, which was still there in the same place. Was she expecting them or was she hallucinating? For a split-second I thought I'd pretend to be Kavita but decided against it.

"I'm Priya, from next door. Remember, I used to come here with my sister?"

Her forehead wrinkled in an effort to remember. A shadow of disappointment hovered on her face. Then after a moment, "Oh right, Priya, of course." She pressed my hand, and then reached for my face and patted my cheek. Gone was the careful formality of earlier times. She used to be loving and kind but was never physically demonstrative. She kept smiling and sizing me up.

"Beta, it has been a long time. I'm so glad to see you."

"Looks like you were expecting someone else. Who are Kavita and Kaveri?"

"How do you know those names?"

"You just . . . ," I held my tongue, realizing her mind and memory might be playing tricks on her.

She patted my hand again and looked at me. There were tears in her eyes. "My girls, they would have been your age . . . " She paused and took a deep sigh.

I waited.

"There was a school shooting. There were nineteen young funerals that day. My heart was in pieces. I decided to leave America. What kind of society celebrates guns!"

"What about your husband?"

"He stayed back."

Sharda Devi wiped her tears. "Anyway, enough of my sob story.

Let me call Mangesh, let's have tea."

"No, no that's not necessary," I said, momentarily forgetting my own trauma that I had come to talk about. Her scars seemed deeper than mine.

"I always wondered why you stopped coming. I had kept a set of books for you to read, it must still be on that shelf over there," she said, pointing to a glass-panelled teak cupboard. "I thought your parents forbade you from coming here, although I could not imagine why. I asked Leela once but she said she did not know." Sharda Devi paused to catch her breath. "How I looked forward to having you over. The lemonade and the readings, your sweet voices and laughter, and the tap of your little feet filled this empty house, and my heart, too." Then she caught herself and looked at her feet; she curled her toes in her leather sandals. "I forget your sister's name," she said, changing the subject.

"Neha."

"Yes, of course, Neha. I hope you've kept up your love of reading. Tell me, how have you been? Are you married? Do you have daughters?" There was a catch in her throat when she said that, and she quickly corrected herself, "Children, I mean?"

"Yes Auntie, two daughters."

"That is so sweet," she said, and took my hand and kissed it. The corners of her eyes filled up with emotion. "They are your jewels, please don't let them out of your sight," she said, pressing my hand tight, as if to underline her words.

I said I lived in Canada and worked as a literary agent helping writers bring their stories to the world, so that people could read them and liberate the words. She chuckled. When I told her that I had started reading to my daughters even when they were in the womb, her eyes sparkled. The solitary figure, who only ten minutes ago had seemed so moribund was now all aglow, happy to have been found.

"I'm so happy you remembered me," Sharda Devi said. "Don't you want to see the books I had kept for you? Why don't you take a look?" she said pointing to the bookcase.

I walked up to the cupboard and opened it, reading the names along the spines as I pulled out each volume with my forefinger. Their covers, stuck together, were reluctant to be pried away after decades of intimate proximity. Dust, humidity and imprisoned words had forged what seemed an unbreakable bond. I picked out an *Alice in Wonderland*. The pages were fragile, almost brittle, and had acquired a brownish tan. A musty smell of ageing paper and stale dead mites greeted me. Oh, the fragrance of old books. I took the book and returned to Sharda Devi.

"I wish I had read them then," I said.

She nodded and turned her gaze toward the window. There was that wistful, faraway look in her eyes again.

"Auntie, you want me to read to you?"

Sharda Devi smiled, wiped a tear from the corner of her eye. She leaned into me and said, "Yes, please do."

Brother's Keeper

My father was tall and skinny with a slight stoop. He had an unlikely flat nose under which an unruly moustache flourished. Dull eyes from sunken sockets looked out at the world and saw nothing agreeable. He ran a small general store in an old hut, which was also where he lived, in a village twenty miles north of town. It was a long distance from home and he visited us once a month. Father had partitioned the hut by hanging up a Sholapuri bedsheet, and slept behind it on a thin cotton mattress and cooked in a corner by the back door. The village square across from the shop was dominated by a large peepal tree under which elders and idlers chatted and smoked bidis for hours on end. Half-naked children played with sticks and discarded bicycle tyres and made a ruckus all day long. The swing that hung from a stout branch was never still; girls and boys jousted with one another to take turns. Beyond the square, a narrow path beaten by human feet led to the shanties.

Every morning Father would lay out the wares on the floor-level platform before the front door and sit behind it, presiding over his paltry dominion. For the villagers, the shop was the only commercial outpost, their only window to the world, with its trinkets, shiny plastic toys and scented soap. These were but a few novelties Father stocked. He kept them locked in a small glass cabinet beside him. Women and children would come and gawk at them lustily. Nobody ever bought them because nobody could afford them. Even essentials like sugar, salt, matches, and oil, as well as lentils, flour, and bidis were sold on credit. Father kept a ledger, and the outstanding dues were paid when villagers came into some money seasonally at harvest time or when casual labourers working in nearby towns returned home on festivals.

Jars of sugar lollies and toffees he kept close to him, away from the reach of the bratty boys who would try to distract him in order to steal from them. He also kept a first-aid kit containing analgesic tablets, cough syrup, cotton swabs, bandages, and a purple tincture that he dispensed for free. Villagers came to him when they ran a high fever, or developed boils or got injured working in the field. It was not uncommon for someone knocking on his door in the dead of the night pleading for relief.

Father was perhaps the only one in the village who wore slippers, and also the only one to possess a radio, a small battery-operated transistor. He turned it on at news time at nine in the morning and a crowd would gather in front of the shop, not to listen to the news but mostly to marvel at the sonorous, disembodied voice coming from the device. The news itself and the world it invoked were out of their reach and caring. The villagers might have felt greater affinity toward the moon and the stars than toward the goings-on beyond the main road. Every few years political heavies came soliciting their votes in exchange for an utopia. The utopia never materialized. The village had no electricity or running water. Time stood still.

When Father came home once a month, he was exhausted from pedalling for the three hours it took him to reach. I would lie in wait for him at the top of the stairs, and my heart would race at his every approaching footfall, and as he came up on the landing I would holler to scare him. It was a childish ritual that had continued from the time I was very small. And every time Father feigned shock and delight.

"How are your studies" was the first thing he asked and every time I gave him the same reply, "Going good."

He would then nod at Mother by way of greeting, and Mother would simply say, "You've come!" Her tone vacillating between a question and a statement.

After he had washed and said his prayers in front of a makeshift altar, Mother would serve him food and sit by his side and talk to him in a low voice. No special dish was made for his visit, nor would it have occurred to either of them that the occasion was in any way special. We lived for the day, day after day. All our todays were like all our yesterdays. There was no notion of the future. Father was content with life and had a sage-like equanimity about the way things were. He never complained about anything.

Naresh, my older brother, on the other hand, complained about everything. He was nineteen, four years older than me, and had inherited his height and build from Father, and bright and pleasant features from Mother. But somehow their faith or fortitude had not passed down to him. He had long spurned God. In his considered opinion, he said, the supernatural being that arranges human affairs could not be unfair. And unfairness, he said, had been stalking him all his life. It began with his birth. He blamed our parents for bringing him into the world—and into a family which could not arrange for even a modicum of happiness for its children, and which, to his endless ire, had accepted this accursed fate with meek resignation. A kind of restlessness ran in his veins. He had no patience for the daily grind of school and considered its scholastic demands pointless. Books are not going to make me rich was his refrain. He dropped out before finishing matriculation much to the displeasure of our parents. "This boy, I don't know what to do with him," Mother would agonize, holding back her tears.

Because Naresh had turned out to be such a bad penny, Mother off-loaded her hopes and dreams on me. "You are my true son," she would say and pat me on my cheek and hug me. "My raja beta will become a doctor," she would add with the earnestness of a believer. This would make me uneasy and I would wonder how she had come to harbour such delusions. Did she have any idea what the world was like out there? Given our spartan means, the most I could hope to become was a stenographer at some mean-minded, penny-pinching, family-owned firm.

Naresh had no such burden to contend with. Free of the family's aspirations, he was like a free bird with no accounting for his comings and goings. He was hardly home, coming only to eat and sleep. He was always taut with anger and whenever he deigned to speak to our parents his words were rude and bitter. When he dropped out of school, Father had chided him gently, "Without education you'll be nothing, beta."

"Is Mahesh Uncle nothing?" Naresh shot back. "And what have you done with your high-school diploma?"

"Money is not everything," Father said softly and went out of the rear door to avoid further exchange. There was never a conversation between the two when Naresh did not bring up Mahesh Uncle to insult Father. Mahesh Uncle was Father's younger brother who had little education but had made lots of money. He lived in a plush bungalow, his daughters went to an English convent school and their family enjoyed every material comfort money could buy. It galled Naresh that the fates and fortunes of two brothers could be so vastly different. To him there was a moral failing in it somewhere.

"They are brothers, for God's sake, how is it that one can allow the other to slip away in such misery and do nothing about it?" Naresh would say in a righteous tone that sounded a little off coming from him. Despite his contempt for Father and his little shack in the village, Naresh was required to swap place with Father at the shop once a month. We had only one bicycle, which Naresh would ride to the shop on a Saturday evening and the next morning Father would bring it home. Naresh's interaction with Father was limited to that one night once a month. It was here they had their arguments, where Father cajoled him to be good and do good, and where Naresh would scoff at him. Father doted on him all the same and bore his disappointment in grim silence. Even when he was with us at home, Father never spoke of Naresh in front of me. I knew that he and Mother talked about him, rueing over his rebellious temperament.

Whenever I tagged along with Naresh to the shop, he would act the older brother and lecture me. He would instruct me about life and its fundamental injustices and explain that people could not be trusted, for they always said one thing and did completely the opposite. He would grumble about our threadbare existence and heap contempt on Father's shop, about which he could not figure out how it made money.

One Saturday evening, as he rode the bike and I sat on the crossbar, he slipped into his mentor mode and began railing as usual against the inequities of the world. "Look how some people have all the money and the rest of us have nothing. They have the best houses, the best chicks, and here we are, reduced to jerking off."

When we reached the shop it was already dark. We ate our supper, which Mother had packed for us, in the light of the kerosene lamp. Afterwards, as Father slept, the two of us sat at the back of the hut and talked softly. Cicadas chirped in the distance and dogs yelped. It was a moonless night and the stars shone brightly.

Naresh puffed on a cigarette deeply and exhaled a plume of smoke with a long sigh.

Father left early the next morning before I awoke. Naresh opened the shop and arranged the boxes and jars and sacks outside and idly waited for custom. I sat inside, resting my back against the wall, from where I could see Naresh's profile. I had brought a book of short stories, *Mansarover* by Munshi Premchand, which I read all morning. There was nothing else to do in the village. Many a time I had attempted to befriend the village boys but they would shrink away, giving me strange looks. I was not sure what it was they did not like about me. Me being upper-caste or just that anyone from the town was alien to them.

As the day progressed people started trickling in to buy small quantities of flour and oil, some asked for matches or an onion or two, a smidgen of salt or a handful of lentils. Their needs were meagre. I could not see the customers from where I sat but could hear their voices. Every time someone came, I was distracted and my ears perked up. I tried to picture the customer by their voice, gauging their age, face, eyes etc. Sometimes the customers came in twos and threes, and it became a challenge to match the voice with the speaker in a consistent manner. At times I was tempted to get up and see if my imagination came any close to the reality. After lunch, late afternoon as I tried to sleep, having put the book aside, I heard a female voice with a sing-song lilt to it. She had come to buy jaggery.

Naresh asked her why she needed jaggery as she was already so sweet. There were giggles in response. Then the voices dropped to whispers. I strained to hear but could not make out anything. Then there was a sudden jangle of bangles and a short, muffled laugh. I imagined Naresh catching her hand and she pulling away swiftly in mock surprise. I hoped there was no one around to witness their coquetry. I never knew Naresh could be so cheesy, and so forward with women. On the road the previous night, he had declared that the world was tight-fisted and nobody was going to give you anything on a platter, that you had to grab what you wanted. Was this what he meant by "grabbing?"

At sundown Naresh closed the shop, and as we finished supper he informed me that a vaudeville troupe was performing Ramlila that evening in the neighbouring village. He urged me to go, he himself was tired and needed to rest. I refused to go by myself. We had an argument and he called me a sissy who could do nothing on his own, but finally he agreed to come.

When we reached the venue, a mile north, the crowd had begun to gather. An improvised stage had been lighted up, powered by a noisy generator behind it. People were sitting on the ground, children taking up the front few rows close to the podium. Men and women kept proprietary distance, women with the ends of their saris partly drawn over their faces. Naresh and I stood at the edge of the audience toward the back. The hum of general chatter was suddenly drowned by a loud banging of drums, then the sharp blare of trumpets rang out. Children shouted in delight and started clapping. The music brought smiles to many faces. Without further ado, the play began. Lord Ram, his wife Sita, and his brother Laxman enter the stage; Ram is banished to a fourteen-year exile in the forest. A male actor playing Sita looked a bit too muscular to be Ram's wife. His movements in the sari were anything but dainty, and when he spoke, mimicking a female voice, he sounded like somebody were garroting him. Children laughed.

The actors hammed and their histrionics were unintentionally burlesque, but no matter, the audience was soon absorbed. Even though the story of the *Ramayan* had been burned into our psyche since birth, the timeless tale of good and evil could never fail to grab our attention. Presently the Hanuman character with a long, arching, stiff tail burst onto the stage and was greeted with a roar of hoots and claps. Somebody let out a piercing whistle. As I looked to my side to see Naresh's reaction, he signalled to me that he was heading back and leaving the bike behind for me. For a split second I thought of joining him but the action on the stage distracted me.

Hanuman with a war cry was swinging his club menacingly, his considerable army behind him ready to do battle, the urgent beat of drums adding to the drama. The monkey god was jumping up and down, bracing for an attack on Lanka, the kingdom of Ravan, to rescue Sita from his clutches. The moment he lunged at the ten-headed ogre, lights went out. There was silence. People thought it was a part of the act. Soon they would see the blood of the vanquished Ravan, his heads smashed to smithereens. The crowd held its breath.

A collective grumble arose when we were told that the generator had broken down. Children began throwing sticks and pebbles at the stage. An old man next to me spat in disgust. As the gathering began to disperse, I walked toward the bicycle. Two boys were already at it, twirling the pedals and banging the spokes against the lock. On seeing me they scooted. I rode back, the tepid night breeze grazing my face. A few villagers were already on their way home; I heard their voices and saw the burning ends of their bidis, whiffs of smoke merging into the night. I sounded the bell, just for kicks, and startled them.

On reaching our hut, I tried to open the door but it did not yield, it seemed to be latched from inside.

I knocked. "Naresh, open," I said softly.

"Who's there!" He seemed surprised. There was a pause, and then muffled, confused voices.

"It's me."

"Already here? So soon?"

"Well . . . "

"Okay, go away, come after some time," he said quickly.

"Go away, where?"

"Don't know. Go now."

Puzzled, I walked around the hut toward the square and sat down under the tree. It was quiet except for the nocturnal noises one hears when all else is quiet. Feeling scared, I focused my gaze on an oil lamp that flickered outside the hut across from the shop. My mind, though, was fixated on Naresh and what he might be up to. Soon I heard voices wafting up from the direction of the road; the people I had passed on the way had caught up. I felt reassured by their presence and watched them walking past until they disappeared into the night.

Not long after, as the last of the stragglers had gone, I heard a tinkle of anklets and hurried footsteps emerging from behind our hut and fading toward the shanties. The next morning as we drank tea and dunked toast-biscuits into our cups, Naresh seemed to be in an especially ebullient mood. He prattled on about how he would start a business and make it big one day. "You can't take life lying down, I tell you that." For the first time he was not raging futilely and seemed to have a plan to actually do something. I nodded as he talked, but the question nagging me was: What was he up to the previous night?

"Why was the door latched?" I asked.

"Latched? When?"

"Last night."

"Hmm . . . don't think so. You know it gets jammed sometimes, you've to push it hard."

"When I knocked, you told me to go away."

"I've no idea what you are talking about."

"Then later I saw someone leaving."

"Looks like you are hearing things and seeing things. There are ghosts here, you know," he said and chuckled.

I said nothing. I had an inkling what he might have been up to and sleep had not come to me easily that night.

Back in town, weeks passed and life lumbered along its daily groove. I saw Naresh only at meal times; he slunk in and out of the house unnoticed. He hardly spoke, his signature sullenness having repossessed him. His enthusiasm over starting a business was short-lived after all. He never mentioned it again. He had become his old self again, except for one noticeable change: he was ever eager to go to the shop on Saturdays. Whenever I asked to go with him, he flatly refused.

A few months later, Mother and I were having supper in the evening when Naresh came running, and as he came up on the landing, his foot caught on the ledge and he stumbled. He swore loudly and, without waiting to catch his breath, said that our shop had burned down. Mother was in shock.

"What about Father?" I asked.

"Don't know. A village fellow who works in the city told me."

Naresh and I left for the village immediately; his friend Atul joined us on another bike. Nobody spoke a word the whole way. The night had turned dark and deep by the time we reached. The stench of smoke lingered in the air. The fire had died down completely. The roof had partly burnt through, and a section of the wall had turned to cinders. The front and back doors were gaping holes and the outer walls were black and charred.

"Where is Papa," I asked.

Naresh did not reply. Atul had the foresight to bring along a candle; he lit it and they stepped inside. I waited outside, praying, not wanting to know what was to come next. For what seemed ages there was silence. Then Naresh emerged, the glow of the candle lighting his face, unnaturally hardened. "Papa is dead," he said plainly. I started crying, fighting the image of his charred body. Naresh and Atul went across the square to a hut to inquire. Atul knocked on the door, a man came out with a lamp. Naresh said something pointing toward the shop. The man appeared angry and gestured with his hand as though shooing them off. Naresh raised his voice and the man slammed the door in his face.

They walked back to where I was sitting. Naresh kicked the dust and cursed the villagers, "Stupid bloody peasants, why can't they tell me what happened?"

"Let's inform the police," Atul said.

Naresh looked at the burnt remains of the shop, and I could see tears welling up in his eyes. Presently we heard noises approaching from the village. We saw a moving glimmer of fire, which turned out to be from the torches the men were carrying. They were ten of them and they came and surrounded us. One of them with a big turban and a thick twirled moustache grabbed Naresh by the collar.

"Motherfucker," he said, seething, teeth grinding. "You think we're playthings for you city loafers."

He pushed him to the ground and kicked him.

When Atul tried to intervene the other men shoved him away, and began jabbing the torches in his face.

Naresh's attacker held him to the ground, his knee pressing on his neck. "If I see you here again, I will burn your pyre here," he said pointing to the gutted shop. Naresh gasped, his eyes bulged. The man punched him in the chest, then he removed his knee, lifted Naresh by the collar and pulled him close to his face. "If the police comes to know, I'll hunt you down and . . . " He threw Naresh back to the ground. As they retreated, the man kept looking back shouting vile curses. Naresh writhed on the ground. He stayed there for a long time whimpering like an injured dog.

The Republik of Sputnik

We hadn't met in twenty years. I wondered in what ways Sunil had changed, if at all. I was pacing the length of the arrival lounge at Bhubaneshwar airport. My palms were sweaty and I had had two coffees already. I had arrived by an early morning flight and Sunil would be flying in later that morning from Kochi. I had my eye on the arrivals board and when his plane landed, I made my way to the exit gate. I spotted him approaching in his familiar measured steps. He was looking straight ahead, indifferent and uncurious. I waved at him. He nodded; his hands were occupied with his bags. As I slapped the side of his arm and enthused about meeting after ages, he responded with just a formal "Hello." When I embraced him, his body stiffened a little at my sudden display of intimacy.

Large and stocky, he tended to suck the air and attention around him and at the same time radiated an aura that repelled people. Despite being older and greyer now, his hair cropped short and moustache drooping, he was the same dour, acerbic curmudgeon. Hard to like and still harder to love. He could be brusque and offensive, and fools inevitably got the short end of his sharp temperament.

We headed to the Airbnb apartment I had rented. As the day progressed, he eased into the familiarity we had shared. We caught up with two decades of life's vicissitudes, reminiscing about old days, laughing over our many follies, remembering forgotten friends and foes. In the evening, after dinner, he rolled a joint. "This is my vice," he said, glancing at me guiltily. His tone was sheepish, a sinner confessing his transgression.

"You mean one of your many vices," I said.

He broke into a laugh, shaking his head. "This is my sputnik. It transports me to outer space." He had been drinking all day, and I would soon learn that he could polish off a bottle of vodka without so much as a burp. "It is the pain, Safdar, the pain of living," he said. "Look around you, so much fuckery going on. You need to steel your heart, fortify your soul." And smiling, he offered me the joint, which I declined.

Sunil always had a grudge against the world. It fell short of his expectations. Obviously his expectations had not changed since we last saw each other, and the world had stubbornly refused to improve. I had met him in a rich and snazzy city on the Persian Gulf. He had joined our magazine's editorial team, whose business apparently was to make celebrities out of idiots. Journalism was a joke in those parts. The media's role was mainly to massage the egos of the rulers. One fine day Sunil said he had had enough of such horseshit. He packed his bags and left, with a promise that we would meet again. It had taken twenty years for us to make good on that promise.

We had reconnected not long ago on social media. On a recent phone call, he suggested taking a trip together to Odisha. He wanted to see the Konark temple. I jumped at the idea before he could change his mind, for it was out of character for Sunil to propose such a venture. Besides, I didn't remember when last I had done anything on an impulse.

As he nursed his sputnik, I suggested we plan the trip.

"I was hoping you would have done the planning," he said.

"This was *your* idea. I thought you knew exactly where you wanted to go, what you wanted to do."

"The only thing I want to do is this," he said, pulling on the joint.

"Incredible!"

"Okay, okay, don't you fulminate. We'll be fine."

We had six days here and no idea how we were going to spend them. I realized that between his booze and his sputnik Sunil had little time for practical matters, so I took it upon myself to organize our days, including first hiring a car with a driver to take us around. The car operator, Kedar, came over to our place to negotiate. He was tall and lanky, with a cheerful face and a silver tongue. He promised a fantastic tour in a new car and with a driver we would be hard pressed to find fault with.

In the morning we came down with our bags. I was excited at the prospect of exploring a part of India I had not seen before. Sunil, too, was chirpy, but only until we saw what Kedar had sent us. The car certainly was new at one time long ago; the driver was big and burly, and his belly stuck out like a pregnant woman's. On seeing us, he frowned. Perhaps he was equally disappointed.

His name was Tito. He looked grouchy and clearly had no love for his job. I told Sunil that we had met his match. He grunted. Tito didn't help with the luggage. He just opened the boot and stood there with his hands in his pockets. We loaded the bags, Sunil cursing under his breath.

I sat behind the driver, whose seat was pushed far back and thrusting into my legs. I asked Tito to pull it forward. He made a show of doing so but did not move a millimetre. Sunil laughed, saying that the poor bastard couldn't help it, his paunch was jammed into the steering wheel. Tito remained unperturbed. He showed none of the obsequiousness that exudes organically from people who spend their lives serving others. I admired his pride, disapproving at the same time his total lack of courtesy and consideration for his passengers.

On our way to Konark, I called Kedar and told him that he had duped us. He laughed as if this were a joke. We spoke in English so Tito wouldn't understand. I told Kedar to either change the car or the driver, and preferably both. He tried to change the subject, but seeing that I would not budge, he hemmed and hawed and said that we were too far from the city for him to send a replacement car. Still, he promised to do something about it. We did not hear from him again.

I could have taken the front seat beside Tito, but it was pushed way forward because Sunil, being large, needed more leg room. My cloistered space became a sore point to bitch about, and Tito became the butt of our jokes. Sunil proved to be unrelenting and highly inventive in his wisecracking. Several times, I had to bend double and clutch my stomach to contain my laughter. Tito, of course, grasped that he was the target of our ribaldry. Sullen and lazy he might have been, but he was no fool. Now and then, I would catch his reflection in the rear-view mirror. His eyes, small and narrow-set, were cold, his chubby face frozen into a sulk.

We made efforts to ingratiate ourselves with him. But Tito remained tight-lipped. Our only window into his world were his phone calls. His mother would call and he would talk loudly and for long stretches. His language—Odiya—we didn't understand, but we recognized a smattering of Bengali words and got a general drift of the conversation. His voice ricocheted like a sonic pinball inside the car. We heard the mother, her voice tinny on the phone's speaker, complaining about his daughter not listening to her, about a neighbour who was beating his wife, about the rising price of lentils, about things big and small that were making her life miserable. At one point, frustrated, she said the entire human race could go to hell. Tito would humour her for a while and then would tell her to calm down. She called up her son four or five times the first day. When they talked, we had to stop our conversation and wait for them to finish. Sunil would be fuming each time Tito answered his phone. The next day, when the phone rang again the first thing in the morning, Sunil made it clear in stern tones that if he needed to talk, he should stop the car and step outside.

We bought two bunches of small bananas, and I gave him one. He accepted the bunch without a smile and ate them one by one, chucking the peels out of the window. I told him not to do that, we should do our bit to keep the roads clean, and someone might easily slip on a peel. He said sorry. But within a few hours he was chucking out peanut shells.

We wanted to empathize with him—obviously he had not been very lucky in the lottery of birth. Our middle-class, guilt-laden sense of privilege chafed at our consciences. "Poor chap, he's had a rough life, maybe there is a reason why he is the way he is," I offered. Sunil agreed. But something about Tito—the way he occupied space, the way the air moved around him, the way he shuffled his flip-flopped feet through the world—something obvious yet hard to put a finger on—kept on irritating us. It irritated us more because we couldn't be sure what it was that was irritating us.

We arrived at the Konark temple. Our guide there, a short plump man, with skin baked the colour of dark chocolate, praised it to the skies. Built on the shore of the Bay of Bengal, this magnificent monument in the shape of a chariot with twelve pairs of wheels drawn by seven horses carved from stone was dedicated to the Sun god, and when the sun was out, the wheels indicated the precise time of day.

"How did they see the time after sundown?" I asked.

"People had better things to do at night," the guide snapped, offended, and pointed to the figurines engaged in sexual congress.

He pointed to a panel far up in the middle of the front façade. "See, doing it from behind." His voice was hushed, conspiratorial. He drew my attention to a threesome here, to a fellatio there, to a cunnilingus over there, taking sophomoric pleasure, as if he was unravelling carnal secrets to a prepubescent schoolboy. "These people were not shy, they did everything openly," he said. "After sunset, of course," he added with a wink.

Sunil was a few paces ahead of me. He did not seem to be particularly awed by the richness or the aesthetics of the carvings. It was only when we were walking back toward the car park that the parade of erotic orgies in stone drew mild praise from him. "How come we became so fucked up? Obviously, something good was going for us there," he said, gesturing toward the temple with his head. "Such art speaks to the genius of a society. Now look around you, there's so much ugliness, stupidity, ignorance."

Tito was smoking and chatting with the other drivers in the car park. Upon seeing us, he started shuffling toward the car. I asked him if he had seen the temple. He hadn't. "It's just a temple," he said. Sunil frowned.

We were on the road again, headed north to the beach town of Gopalpur. The countryside was intermittently green, the fields devoid of new crop, and for some reason all the electric poles we passed were tilted at an angle. Tito didn't know why. We passed through villages with mud huts, crowned with thatched roofs. We saw solid, narrow buildings of brick, two and three stories tall, and less than six feet wide. This, we noticed, was a common feature in the rural parts we were travelling through. "Imagine, everybody has to sleep lengthwise," Sunil remarked. "What devilish minds would create these rows of recesses and call them houses?" He grunted and gazed out the window.

After a while, he said, "We should start our own Republik, republik with a K. It should include four southern states. Secede from the north, the ignorant and fascist cow belt. We'll call it the Republik of Sputnik."

"And you will be the dictator of the new Republik?" said I, my face deadpan.

His smile was partly hidden under his bushy moustache. "Dictatorship will be necessary in the beginning, to consolidate the fledgling nation, but when it is able to stand on its feet, we will institute democracy and submit the state to the will of the people."

Will of the people. The words had a surreal ring to them.

"Looks like we're dreaming up another utopia?"

"We have to start with a dream, Safdar, with an ideal. Things are never going to be perfect. But we have to start somewhere. Smaller area, fewer people, educated people."

He took a swig from his flask and wiped his moustache with his hand. His eyes were spry, pupils dancing. Gazing at nothing in particular, he enumerated all the good things the Republik would bring into the world—a roof over every head, food in every mouth. Free education and full employment and an equitable distribution of wealth. And the things that would be banished. "No army and no police. They are the unnecessary evils on which I won't spend even a demonetized rupee." He went on to name some prominent writers and intellectuals and leaders he admired, who would be granted honorary citizenship. There was something touching and vain about a grown man daydreaming of a better world. It was so unlike him.

I asked Tito to pull up to the side. We stopped at the edge of a vast open field, its crop young and drenched in sunlight. I needed to pee. Sunil also helped himself. Then he lit up a joint, away from the car in the shade of a tree. I saw Tito eyeing him curiously while scratching his privates. I walked up to him and started chatting.

He exploded with laughter when I told him about the Republik. For the first time, I saw him relaxed, and suddenly everything about him was softer, gentler, more likeable. He said he hadn't heard such a funny joke in a long time. I told him he should laugh more often, it suited him. He stopped and eyed me suspiciously, wondering if this was another dig at him.

We reached the hotel in Gopalpur. Run by the ministry of tourism, it was quite well appointed for a government outfit. A humongous ledger took up the entire front desk. I entered our details in it, my pen moving across a never-ending row, and Sunil made a snarky remark about government bureaucracy. The clerk looked at him uncomprehendingly. We went up to our room. It had a balcony facing the Bay in the distance. A faint roar of the waves reached us.

After a rest, we walked down toward the beach with two bottles of chilled beer. We discovered that we were at an elevation; a sandy slope ran down to the water. Up here were a few stone chhatris—canopies—for visitors to sit. In one of them was a young couple pretending to be undisturbed by our sudden presence. We occupied the canopy at the front and opened the bottles. It was windy and humid; the salty air was soothing, the chilled beer satisfying. My eyes strayed toward the couple, now in an intimate act, the girl straddling the guy's knees. I looked away and loped down toward the water. Sunil wanted to be left alone with his sputnik.

There was nobody else around. I walked along the shifting line where the waves washed up. The sun was on the wane, the tide was low, the ocean still churning. The shore stretched ahead of me as far as the eye could see. Fishing boats, worn and weather-beaten, were lined up like beached whales. I was alone and suddenly felt one with the water, the earth, the sky. Something stirred in the soul and I sensed an epiphany rising. But a wave scrambling up and embracing my feet broke into my stillness. Wet sand squelched beneath my tread, tiny baby crabs scurried away into their holes. The dusk was deepening, the sky aflame in colours that defied the imagination. Further ahead, some fishermen were hauling a boat out of the sea. It looked like the boatman had been tardy in getting back to shore and been caught in the low tide.

I stood and watched the fishermen struggle. The boat was a large wooden canoe. A dozen or so men, sunburnt and sinewy, waited for the next wave to lift and propel the boat forward, so they could give it their all. Every heave came with a loud chorus of grunts. They progressed a few feet at a time. I considered giving them a hand but banished the idea instantly. My mollycoddled, city-bred body would not make an ounce of a difference. I resumed my walk, and on my return, almost an hour later, they had just managed to park the boat. Across from the shore I could see a cluster of thatched huts, where human silhouettes flitted about. Children's hoots rang out and smoke wafted up from woodfires.

It was dark now and the rumble of the waves had subsided into a gentle hum that sounded like a lullaby. I climbed back up to the canopy where I had left Sunil. He said that the sputnik and the sea breeze had transported him to a magical world, and pitied me for missing out on such a numinous experience. I boasted that such temporary forays into transcendence were not for me, I was one for everlasting enlightenment. "That, my dear Watson, is an illusion," he quipped. Back in the hotel, we made ourselves comfortable on the balcony and ordered room service. Half-way thorough the meal, Sunil got up and went to bed, the magical world claiming him at last.

The next morning Tito seemed grumpier than usual; eyes puffed up, hair cow-licked, his dirty grey Bermuda shorts on the verge of slipping from his waist. He said he'd had to sleep in the car. The room that the hotel staff had given him was under construction, strewn with concrete and sand and tins of paint and pails of plaster. "Even a dog would not sleep in there," he said. You should have told us, I said. He shrugged, as if to say, as if you care. And the truth was, we didn't really. Kedar had made it clear that Tito's lodging was his problem. But still, I felt bothered by the fact that he'd had such a rough night. Every time we checked into a place, we had enquired whether there was any sleeping arrangement for the driver. Mostly there was none, and beyond that formality we had done nothing. Tito continued to sleep in the car, reclining his seat all the way down. In the mornings, I would find him recumbent, snoring with abandon.

Feeding him was our responsibility. We gave him money for a meal, or where possible, he would eat at the same place as us. He was free to order whatever he liked and he had quite an appetite. He has to satisfy the beast in that belly, Sunil remarked. We didn't know his caste nor did we care, but we were acutely aware of his class. For all our high-minded sensibilities and egalitarian urges, we did not invite him to join us at our table. And much to our relief, we found the same hesitation in him. He too preferred to eat by himself, and while eating, he was constantly on his phone. "He is either consuming porn or propaganda," said Sunil, then asked, "You know why the internet is so cheap in India?" I shook my head. "It is a weapon of mass distraction. The masters cannot do their work until the serfs are consumed by their phones, by WhatsApp and TikTok and whatnot."

"So, no social media in the Republik, then?" I needled him.

"Absolutely not. We will establish agoras for public debate, out in the open and free. No digital bullshit."

Tito seemed less grouchy then on, but still his congenital laziness persisted. He still did not help us with the luggage unless we asked him to; he would not speak until he was spoken to. There was a coldness, a reserve about him which was hard to breach.

There were giant hoardings of Prime Minister Narendra Modi at every major traffic junction. Wanting to test Sunil's theory about internet propaganda, I praised Modi, extolled his achievements and his leadership. Tito glanced at me from the rear-view mirror with a look of suspicion that I was quite familiar with by then. I remained poker-faced. He smiled. All politicians are crooks, he said.

I looked at Sunil. "Obviously, Tito's into porn," he said.

I pressed on and told Tito that he was wrong, that Modi was a great leader. Just look at what he had done—and I listed his party's talking points. Tito countered each with a laugh. He knew I was leading him on and did not bother to refute. I then goaded him about Biju Patnaik, the former chief minister who was revered in Odisha like a demigod, with every other monument and institution named after him. Sunil said they should have named the whole bloody state after him, thus saving a whole lot of expense and trouble. Tito pooh-poohed Patnaik, saying that his family had done really well but not the people. "Look," he said, pointing to the shacks under the politician's huge statue. I again looked at Sunil. He gave a thumbs-up, beaming. "Tito's brain is stunningly unwashed. I declare him the first citizen of the Republik," he said.

In Puri, we were staying at the house of a former diplomat, who had rented out his ground-floor rooms. Our room had just one king-size bed. This was quite contrary to our expectation. When we had booked, the picture had shown two beds. We complained to the owner. He apologized and said that this was the only room available. To allay our disappointment, he made small talk and asked what brought us to Odisha. I am a travel writer, Sunil lied. The man suddenly sat up erect, perhaps anxious that he might get a bad review. With a hint of pride, he told us that he had been an ambassador to many countries. Sunil remained unimpressed. Later he confided, "Saw how he was trying to feel important, as if he could curry immunity from my pen."

The bed took up most of the room. I folded a sheet lengthwise and placed it along the middle of the bed. This is our Line of Control, the Laxman Rekha, I said. Sunil ignored me. His mind was occupied with a more urgent matter. He went out, enquired with the attendant and came back grinning. The booze store was just round the corner, he announced. He looked at the partitioned bed and then at me. "You're straighter than I thought," he said with amusement.

Breakfast the next morning was sumptuous—omelettes, idlis, medu vadas, plain yoghurt, and a hot piping cup of masala chai. We polished everything clean. Sunil grudgingly admitted that the ambassador was not a bad chap after all. After a shave and a shower, he looked rejuvenated and ready for the day. Tito said we were late for the Jagannath Temple. He dropped us off in a side street, as cars were not allowed near the temple complex. We walked about a hundred metres, emerging into an open square, and were greeted by the imposing temple. The vast, paved grounds were swarming with people. Tito was right, we were late. Sunil appeared repulsed by the scene and said he couldn't go inside; he had a phobia of crowds and crowded places. I told him he would be risking the displeasure of Lord Jagannath and was dismissed with a flick of the hand. I asked him to mind my shoes and walked through a heavy security cordon toward the entrance. I looked back but had already lost sight of Sunil. I despaired for my shoes.

At the temple gate, I was accosted by priests pestering me with their services, like touts outside a cricket stadium. Priests in full white or saffron wraparounds—a single piece of cloth draped around the waist and the trailing portion slung over the shoulders—sat cross-legged with their tools of trade and tchotchkes neatly arranged before them. A few of them were in deep conference with their customers, mostly married couples.

Inside, the temple was packed with devotees, the air was thick with the smell of burnt oil, sweat, and fervent prayer. The precinct was large, dark, and damp, with the seat of the Lord in the middle. Given the size of the temple and its reputation, the idol was quite small. I went around the sanctum, made a small prayer and exited from a side door. There were quite a few other smaller satellite temples in the complex, and devotees were rushing to them one after the other, eager to propitiate all the deities. I reflected that the religious impulse has been with us since the dawn of time. I strolled around, feeling detached from the scene, wondering why I did not feel the need to believe, why that impulse had evaded me. And yet I had said a prayer.

I made my way down the steps toward the exit. I found my shoes. Sunil had abandoned them and was sitting on a stone bench away from the gate. He said he had been enjoying from his perch the human dilemma typical of our postmodern age. How people reacted with shock and confusion when the security crew told them that mobile phones were not allowed inside. "Humans will always be slaves, to technology, to gods, to whatnot," he said. I braced myself for the volley of unsolicited wisdom. "Chhey," he grunted. "For how long has life been around? Three, four billion years? And this is what we have evolved up to?" he gestured toward the crowds with a slight nod of his head. "We would've been better off as monkeys."

I extended my hand and pulled him up on his feet. "Well, a monkey with a smart phone is better than a monkey with a banana," I said. Sunil frowned. "Your thinking, my dear Watson, is quite pedestrian."

We found Tito by the car, looking agitated. He said the car had broken down—maybe the battery had died. He wanted us to push it to get it into motion, so that he could get the engine going. We cursed Kedar and got behind the car. The next instant, Tito took the driver's seat. "What!" Sunil exclaimed. "Is he out of his mind? I'm not going to push this baby elephant." He took his hands off the car and I followed suit. We stood there, not sure what to do next. Tito looked at us from the rear-view mirror, urging us to push. We shook our heads. "What's the matter?" he asked, stepping out. Sunil was blunt; he said it was impossible to move the car with him in it. Tito wrung his hands, as if to ask, "Do you have a better solution?"

Sunil told me to take the steering and asked Tito to push. Tito was not amused. When he had asked us to push the car, he could barely hide his smugness.

The car started moving. I saw that a couple of passersby had joined to push, making this a public enterprise. I shoved the stick into second gear. The engine shuddered, gave up, and then rasped and snorted and came to life. I remained at the steering and we drove off. Tito sat behind me, twisting himself into the cramped space I had been occupying so long. I asked him if the seat was comfortable. He kept mum, reeking of sweat and, I suspect, rage.

The next morning, after Tito had the car repaired, we headed back to Bhubaneswar. Sunil was sober now and a bit contrite. Last night we'd had an argument about his drinking, and he had told me to shut up. "You're not my bloody wife and stop acting like one." The words had stung. Telling him to fuck off, I had gone for a walk and stayed out for a long time. For all his hard exterior, I realized that he was soft and sensitive inside. Fragile too. He got flustered by small worries, by the little things. Sleep did not come easily to him. He liked to arrange his affairs with care, well in advance; he did not like surprises. He had never married. I wondered if having a family would have given him a sense of rootedness, helped anchor his angst in the love and care of close ones, obviated the need for drinking, or whether the banality of married life would have frazzled him further and intensified his unease with life and living. There was a struggle in him, the drinking quietening the demons only temporarily. I wanted to help, but was not sure how.

It was another gorgeous day, warm and bright. The traffic was light and Tito was playing Hindi songs on the stereo. Sunil asked me to ask him to look for a booze shop. Some nerve he had. But I knew he was trying to gauge my mood. Ask him yourself, I snapped. Tito listens to you, he flattered. I frowned.

"Okay, okay. You know what Tito calls you?" he asked. I did not respond.

"He calls you Police-sir," he said, and started laughing. "Even he knows you're a bloody stick-in-the-mud."

"Hmm, *that* is rich," I said and looked at Tito in the rear-view mirror. Having fathomed the gist of the conversation, he was smiling guiltily. "No, no, sir, Sunil sir is lying."

Somehow, I had started to find this roly-poly oaf endearing—his round pudgy face, small eyes glinting with mischief, his thin moustache with uneven sides, his unruly mop of hair, his chequered, tight-fitting shirt—and was secretly pleased that he had an opinion about me. I told him that this police-sir would beat the shit out of him, true to police tradition. He chortled, "What sir?" I had a feeling that Tito and Sunil were in cahoots and had way more in common than one would suspect. Their relationship had been rocky from the start; the two sourpusses had hated the sight of each other. Now, in a matter of a few days, they were sharing confidences. Who would have thought?

In Bhubaneswar, we headed to our lodging for the night. Tito came in the morning to take us to the Khandagiri and Udaygiri caves, situated between two hills. Sunil said that he had no interest in seeing these ancient hovels, he had no energy or desire to climb hills and would sit it out.

"Coming here was your idea, and you keep on having cold feet?" I said.

"All this ancient history is coming out of my ears," he said impatiently.

The Khandagiri caves with the Digambar Jain Temple at the summit were open to the public for free, and as such, the hill was littered with trash. I quickly went up the broad-stepped path and said a quick prayer at the temple. There were caves on the way, crumbling and graffiti-ridden, and in some of them, instead of monks, lovers had found refuge from the prying samsara.

The Udaygiri caves complex charged a fee and, as a result, was better maintained. The gardens around it were manicured and lush. I hired a guide to take me around. We walked from cave to cave, the guide explaining the significance of each. I poked my head into them and, more than once, found bodies locked in communion. The hovels still have their use, Sunil would be glad to know, I thought. I went up the hill to the plateau; from here, the sprawling city was visible brightly toasting in the afternoon heat. I spotted the Shanti Stupa in the south-east—a white pagoda on a hill where King Ashoka had realized the futility of war after the exceptionally gory Kalinga War that had turned the Daya river red with blood. Ashoka's edicts, expressing remorse and advocating nonviolence, were carved in stone, and on stone they had remained, ignored by modern, shining India. Sunil was right, how did we come to be so fucked up?

Back in the street, I looked for my companions, wondering what they might be up to. I found them in the car with the doors on one side wide open. Tito was sitting sideways with his feet on the ground. He saw me first and alerted Sunil, who grinned like a Cheshire Cat.

"Never knew you'd be so happy to see me," I taunted.

"Chhey! You are delusional," he said, his speech sounding slurred.

"Looks like you two are getting along swimmingly," I complained in a mock-injured tone.

Tito mumbled, "Police-sir, police-sir," guilt written all over his face. He too was in a good mood, loose of tongue and taking liberties with me, teasing me, albeit cautiously. I wondered what had transpired in my absence to turn these two grumpy misanthropes into models of good cheer.

I didn't have to wonder for long. As we drove, Sunil explained, tripping over his words. He and Tito had got talking and the conversation had veered inevitably to sputnik. Sunil had asked Tito if he could use his connections to procure some weed. Meaning to be ironic, he had taken a wild shot. But without blinking an eyelid, Tito had reached under his seat to retrieve a small plastic container and inside it, wrapped in layers of newspaper, was his stash. He gave it to Sunil, who by now was in a state of shock, not believing that Tito—this down-at-heel, woebegone man, this surly, uncouth, crotchety slacker—would be so resourceful as to conjure sputnik out of thin air.

"And this stuff, I tell you Safdar, is gooooood, unbelievable. As unbelievable as this oaf being in possession of it." Sunil's eyes were watering with laughter, his reserve and grouchiness melting in the pot.

"Good for you," I said, trying to bring his enthusiasm down a notch or two.

He had not cared to ask how my visit to the caves had been. His eyes were closed, a smile hovering on his lips and peeking through his moustache. I was happy for him, and in a way, envied the calm that had settled on him. We were on our way to the lodging. It was our last day. Tomorrow we were flying out.

Tito's phone rang. He picked it up. When he had finished talking, he pulled the car to the side and turned toward us. It was his mother, it was urgent, he would have to go home. His face was bloated with worry; his eyes were narrow and jaundiced. "Your place is in a different part of the town, and my house is in the opposite direction. I can't drop you first. Either you come with me or take a taxi."

Sunil and I exchanged looks. Before I could say anything, Sunil told him that we would go with him. Tito made a U-turn and zinged through the traffic. He hadn't exhibited such alacrity in the past five days. By the time we reached his house, dusk was beginning to fall, and Sunil was in La-La Land. I shook him awake.

"Where are we?" he asked.

"We've just arrived at the gates of heaven," I said.

"Chhey, I was there before you woke me up. Tito, this bastard, why does he have to drive so fast?"

Tito had already slammed the door behind him and was striding across an unpaved path toward a long tenement building with a series of doors facing the front. The structure looked half-finished and had never seen a lick of paint. An old woman was sitting in the doorway. She gestured inside the house, and Tito rushed in. I sprinkled some water on Sunil's face. "Let's see what's going on." He grumbled and struggled out of the car and followed me.

By now some neighbours had trickled out from their homes to gawk at us and started chattering among themselves. Sunil and I came to stand by the door where Tito had entered. The old woman did not seem to notice us. We peeked inside. In the unlit room Tito was squatting on the floor by a girl, his daughter I presumed. The habitation was just this one room. The corner on the left was crammed with a kerosene stove and pots and pans. On a low shelf above were clear plastic jars with red lids, their sides opaque with dirt. Bedding was piled up against the opposite wall, where the girl lay. There were clothes hanging from nails on the walls.

"What happened?" I asked.

The old woman appeared startled. "Who's this?" she shouted, staring blankly in our direction. Looks like she is blind, I whispered to Sunil.

"Uma, my daughter, she had a fit," said Tito. "She's okay now. The neighbour came and made her smell this piece of leather. We keep it just for this kind of emergency."

"Have you taken her to a doctor?" Sunil asked.

"She has a devil inside her. What can a doctor do?" The old woman interjected. Then, addressing Tito, she asked, "Who are these people?"

"Mai, they're my passengers. They were with me when you called," said Tito. Then, turning to us, he said, "My mother, she's blind."

"You must take your daughter to a doctor," I said.

"Doctor-voctor can do nothing!" the old woman shouted. "It's the spirits. God knows whose sin this fool has brought home."

"Mai, shut up!" Tito yelled and stepped out and walked toward the car. He stopped by the curb and waited for us. "My mother can be rude, but she's right . . . Uma is not my daughter." It seems, by some bizarre quirk of events, a woman he had been friendly with had accused him of fathering the girl and had dumped the baby on him. He hadn't found a way to refute her claim. "I could not throw her on the street. Mother has accepted her but always goes on and on about evil spirits." Tito fell silent, eyeing the children who had gathered around us. He hollered at them to move away.

"I don't know if it is spirits or not," he added, "but I can't afford to go to a doctor, and then there will be tests and medicine. Why bother when a piece of leather works fine."

"How often does it happen," asked Sunil.

"Once in two months or so. Sometimes more, sometimes less."

"The longer you leave it untreated the worse it becomes, you know that?" Sunil said. "And it is not spirits, it's a disease of the brain. My cousin used to have it, but after treatment his seizures have almost disappeared."

Tito was hardly listening. He took his seat behind the wheel. Sunil and I kept standing on the edge of the footpath. Don't bother taking us home, I told him. You be with your daughter. We will take a taxi.

"No, no," he said. "My duty, my duty."

"Your duty right now is your daughter, take care of her."

Sunil pulled out a wad of notes and handed it to him. He looked at Sunil, puzzled. "No Sir. No, no . . . I'm okay."

"Take it Tito, you'll need it."

"No Sir, you'll be gone tomorrow, and this money will be spent, and then what?"

Sunil riffled the notes idly and looked around as though searching for something. "This is for the stuff you gave me, okay?" he finally said.

Tito looked at the notes for a long while then pulled out a couple and thanked him. Sunil shook his head and returned the bundle to his pocket. He patted Tito on the shoulder. "Hope your daughter feels better."

We hailed a taxi and took his leave. Both of us were quiet. I looked out the window. Lights had come on in the shops; people were out and about, lolling, chatting, going about their business, eating at roadside stands.

The taxi stopped at a red light. A young girl came scampering to Sunil's window. She was hawking clay replicas of the Jagannath Temple. "Take the blessing of the Lord with you, Sir," she said, and kept repeating it like a mantra, her eyes pleading more than the words. Sunil took a piece from her, reached into his pocket and gave her a note. The girl was shocked at the large denomination, and said she did not have change. Sunil told her to keep it. The taxi pulled away.

"Interesting purchase," I said.

"For the Republik. We need to launch it on an auspicious note," said Sunil, his voice barely audible. It was dark and I couldn't see his face.

Open Season

It had rained all night. The grass was still wet and the ground was soft as clay. Bush and nettle had overgrown the area between the graves, colonizing every spare inch, and neem and peepal trees stood like mighty sentinels guarding the dead. The occasional gust of breeze released a shower of rainwater from the leaves overhead.

Mother, frail and shrunk with age, picked her way among the graves, one hand lifting the hems of her salwar from the wet earth, while adjusting the gauzy dupatta on her head with the other. Her sparse, henna-dyed hair had not seen a comb since the day of the tragedy. Father walked a few steps ahead in ill-fitting cotton pants and an old, checked shirt carelessly tucked in. He walked as if he had lost his way.

I followed them at a distance. They had not had the time to grieve in peace; scenting a meaty story in our public tragedy, a media horde had descended upon us like hyenas. And so the calmness of the cemetery came as a welcome reprieve. Upon reaching the grave, Father stood at its head, looking down at it, mumbling prayers to himself. He had not been talking much.

The grave—an elongated mound of earth—was fresh, though the flowers strewn upon it from the previous day had been squished by the rain; rose petals floated in little pools of muddy water. Mother secured her dupatta around her head and squatted beside the grave, shedding silent tears, fingering the rose petals as though to read clues to the unthinkable that had befallen us. She dipped her fingers into the loose wet earth and hesitated. Sensing that she wished to kiss the grave and say a prayer, Father took out a crumpled handkerchief and spread it before her. Mother gingerly put her fingers down on the ground beside her for support, and lowered her head on the handkerchief and started violently sobbing.

"Enough, Mariam, enough," said Father.

I squinted up at the sun peeking out through the moving clouds. A crow shrieked somewhere in the neem tree above. Placing my hands gently on my mother's shoulders, I helped her sit up.

"Ya Allah, what sins have we committed?" Father lamented. "Why are you punishing us?"

I patted his back. "Abba, please . . . ," I wanted to say, but the words caught in my throat. I wanted to say, have sabr, be patient. But what solace could one invoke for a father maddened by sorrow?

The mob had come armed with sticks and rage, bloody murder in their eyes. Our small, dusty town would have fallen off the map in due course because of its obscurity and insignificance, but my brother Khalid's killing changed all that. I came to know of it on TV news. It cannot be true, was my first impulse. In our town, Muslims were a minority, but we had lived in peace with our Hindu neighbours for generations and more.

I watched as the reporter shoved a microphone in my mother's face and asked in a cheery tone, "How do you feel after the death of your son?" *Death*. Not murder, not lynching. Mother just wept.

A Muslim man had been killed by a mob, the news anchor said. She neglected to mention that the mob was Hindu.

—

Every year, on Diwali day, our Hindu neighbours sent us sweets. Our father would already have bought us firecrackers and sparklers for the festival. On Diwali night, after homework and supper we would troop out into the street, twirling our sparklers, making loops and zigzags, tearing the air with fire, shouting hoots of delight. A fountain would erupt somewhere, blinding us with its brilliance; a ground-spinner would suddenly whizz into our path; a rocket stuck into a bottle would swoosh up into the air. It was all so exciting. The peal of our laughter was not Muslim; the glint in our eyes was not Hindu.

Our neighbour's daughter, Sarita, would make beautiful rangoli patterns with coloured chalk outside our front door, and Mother placed oil lamps on the rangoli for three nights. We had grown up seeing our father decorate his shop with lights and oil lamps to welcome the goddess Lakshmi. For the longest time when I was young, I did not realize that Diwali was a Hindu festival. And when I did, it made no difference.

But two years ago, when the local shopkeepers' association went from shop to shop collecting donations for Diwali decorations, they did not come to our shop. The three men who went around, whom Father knew very well, went past without even a greeting. Father shut the shop early that day, arriving home very agitated. "Are they ignoring me because I'm Muslim? Don't we celebrate Diwali? Don't they see the lights I put up every year? The sweets I distribute?"

As Diwali approached, he would order dozens of boxes of

sweetmeats, which would be wrapped in shiny paper and tied with coloured threads, and distributed them around. Father would go himself to greet the more important clients in their homes. Sometimes I would tag along. Mother would dress me up in my best clothes as though it were Eid. We were greeted with utmost respect and offered sweets and cold drinks. Father had always had a beard, its colour changing from black to copper with the years. He would wear a lacy skullcap and looked distinctly Muslim. But on these occasions his appearance or faith never mattered. He would embrace his clients and greet the women of the house with joined hands, addressing them as bhabhis. Who could have suspected that his business neighbours would rebuff him because of his religion?

Father took the insult to heart. But he was not one to sit back and sulk like a schoolboy shunned by his playmates. On the eve of Diwali, he hired two men and built a huge bamboo arch in front of his shop. It was draped in multicoloured saris, which were then hung with hundreds of light bulbs. He decked the shop front with earthen oil lamps. On Diwali night, the shop stood out like a jewel, the brightest on the street, and word quickly spread. Passersby gaped in wonder at the illumination. When they discovered that the owner—Father—was a Muslim, they were first confused, then a little surprised. Some congratulated him. The shopkeepers got the message bright and clear. The next day, they came to apologize.

But when Khalid was killed, nobody came. So much had changed in such a short time.

—

A few years ago, when I first took a job in Delhi, I had a hard time renting a room. Decent, middle-class folks would show me their house and discuss the rent and house rules, but when they heard my name, they would suddenly go cold. Some bluntly told me they didn't want a Muslim as a tenant. At long last, Surinder Khurana, a Punjabi Hindu widower, opened his doors to me.

Khurana sahab was a big, hirsute man, with a well-trimmed salt-and-pepper beard and shoulder-length hair, which he had the habit of sweeping back with his hand every few minutes. A retired army colonel, he was warm and charming. His heart was left of centre, he told me. And that's where it ought to be, I had replied with a chuckle. That, I guess, sealed our friendship. On Saturday evenings, over Old Monk and roasted peanuts, he would regale me with tales of army officers, their wives, their liaisons and other shenanigans. A commanding personality, he was not afraid to speak his mind, and his tongue would loosen in direct proportion to the number of glasses he had put back. He had a way with words and used his husky voice to good effect. Few women could have resisted his charms, I thought, and imagined that he must have had his own share of peccadillos.

He told me about the scams that permeated every level of the military—from arms deals to the procurement of booze to the supplies of boot polish. "What would people *not* do to land an army contract?" he would say. "Palms are greased and arses licked all the way from the cantonment to the parliament, and all the way back. My dear man, the people—the civilians as we call them—are being gamed, and the funny thing is that they think this is democracy."

For an establishment man, he sounded a bit too radical and cynical. I felt uneasy when he told me tales about the bravery of Muslim men in uniform. Why do liberals feel the need to reassure us of our patriotism? Once he noticed my discomfort and was quiet for a while. The bitter taste of rum lingered on my tongue. A parrot flew out of a nearby tree in a green blur.

Khurana sahab took a large sip and smacked his lips. "Religion is a curse on the human race. And sorry to say, you Muslims are full of shit, with your fatwas and your burqas. And these idiot Hindus want to be like you. Banning this, banning that. Turning cow-*ma* into a dogma. Height of stupidity." He took another large sip. "The India of Gandhi and Nehru is a distant dream. No hope. Instead evil clowns have taken over."

The residents of the building were particularly upset that he had rented a room to a Muslim. One morning, a group of people came to his door and handed him a letter. I was at the kitchen table having breakfast and could hear them speaking in low voices. A couple of them craned their necks to stare at me. Khurana sahab read the document and, after a moment, tore it up and threw it in their faces. Then he slammed the door shut. I asked him what that was all about, but he just shook his head and said, "Nothing." Then he took a few paces and hissed, "The bastards, what audacity!" He did not elaborate further, and I did not ask.

The night watchman filled me in with the details. I would go down after supper to smoke and he would bum cigarettes from me. He told me that the building committee had wanted to oust me but Khurana sahab had told them to buzz off. They were pretty rattled. Now whispers were circulating—that Khurana was up to no good—that his tendencies were suspect. Why were his tenants always young men? And all his servants, too? The watchman waited for me to say something. I simply smiled and exhaled a plume of smoke into the night.

If I were to tell this to Khurana sahab, he would have been thoroughly amused. "Good for them, let these shitheads stew in their gossip," he would have said with a characteristic loud guffaw. He probably already knew the reputation he had among the residents and could afford to ignore it. But I—an outsider, a tenant, a Muslim—could feel the heat of hostility in their stares, in their silences, in the way they would stop talking when they saw me coming, or move out of my path, in the whispers behind my back. My walk from the flat to the building's gate made me acutely self-conscious. My Muslimness felt like a burden—like something illegitimate, a crime, something I ought to be ashamed of. I kept my gaze low. Only the pull of a cigarette drew me out and down into the compound, for Khurana sahab wouldn't allow me to smoke in the balcony. In the three years that I lived there, I don't think I ever spoke to anyone else in that building except the night watchman.

—

The evening I heard the news of my brother's slaying, Khurana sahab was with me in the drawing room. When I told him it was my mother the reporter was talking to on TV, and it was my elder brother Khalid who had been killed, he thought at first that I was joking. "No, no, this cannot be," he said when the truth sank in. He suddenly slid back on the couch, his hands covering his face. "No, no, no," he mumbled.

The lynching of people transporting cattle had made the news every few weeks, but I could never have imagined that this scourge could work its way to my home in a middle-class neighbourhood. My brother was an accountant and Father's shop sold utensils. All had seemed well. It was more than two years since beef had been banned in our state, and we had switched to eating mutton. The truth is that the beef we ate was buffalo meat and not cow meat, and we were not very fond of it either. We would eat it only because it was cheaper than mutton. Goat meat was for the rich folks. The only connection Khalid had with cow meat was that he worked for a beef exporting company owned by a Hindu.

I sat there unable to cry, unable to feel anything. In the news, my mother appeared numb, too shocked to make sense. She was in the front veranda of our house, alone and confused. I wondered where my father was. The media people were crowding her from all sides and two constables on the edge of the throng were smiling proudly at the camera. I suddenly felt afraid for my family. I wished someone would disperse the mob and let my mother breathe.

Khurana sahab wiped his face with his shirt sleeve and put his hand on my shoulder. "Go to your family, there's no time to waste. They need you." He did not say anything more. The flamboyant anger and the torrent of abuse such an incident might have provoked were missing. His ramrod straight posture had suddenly become lax. He seemed finally to be giving up on the India of his dream.

He asked his driver to drop me at the bus station. I would be in time to take the night bus. I quickly packed and was ready to go. Khurana sahab embraced me at the door.

I could not sleep a wink on the bus. There had been lynchings and attacks on Muslims in recent years as though it were open season. And before this virulent phase hundreds—thousands—had been massacred in so-called communal riots. But none of those atrocities had affected me directly. I would vent my rage among like-minded people—more recently on social media—and despair at the state of affairs. Then the anger would subside until the next atrocity, and the next, *and* the next. Finally it had caught up with me. They had killed my brother. For what? For possessing beef? That could not be. Surely there had been a mistake—a huge mistake. Maybe the mobs had mistaken him for someone else. I wished it were someone else they had killed. I cried silently in the dark that night on the bus.

I arrived home late in the morning. The street was deserted, and our house looked ravaged. The front door was broken, the windowpanes smashed, rocks and sticks and garbage were strewn on the porch. I walked in warily, my heart thumping. Alone in the front room, Mother was sitting on the floor. She had been reading the Quran, and seemed to have nodded off. I approached her quietly, dropped on my knees before her and took her hand. She opened her eyes and, without a word, started weeping. I too was unable to hold back my tears. I embraced her and her bony frame shook in my arms. She paused to ask if I had eaten. "Oh, Ammi," I lied, "yes, I have eaten."

"Where's Abbu?" I asked. He had gone to the cemetery. "And by now Khalid must be in the ground," she said. She started weeping again, violently. It was too late to go for the burial, and I sat down beside my mother, back against the bare wall, holding her hand.

How happy Khalid was the last time I saw him, a year ago. He had just bought a shiny new red beast, a Bajaj Pulsar. He took me for a ride and through his helmet, his voice partly losing itself in the wind, enumerated the bike's many features—the power of its engine, its superior torque and high rpm. It was, of course, very stylish. He was proud of it.

Khalid was ten years older than I and like all good elder brothers, concerned very much about my future. He had not liked it when I took up a job at a call centre in Delhi, having failed to find anything better despite completing my engineering degree with distinction. I had assured him that the job was only temporary, to keep myself busy until something more suitable came along. It was five years since then and I had drifted far away from my field of study. I worked on American time, taking calls from irate customers with malfunctioning appliances. It was mind-numbing routine and my circadian cycle was so messed up that all I could do was eat, sleep, and work, my days and nights blending into each other in a seamless loop. That last time we met, when he took me for a ride, we stopped at the local paan shop and over chai Khalid gave me an ultimatum:

"You have a year to find a new job."

I looked at him and raised an eyebrow.

"Or else you come home."

Mother had fallen quiet; her eyes were closed. Presently Razia, my sister-in-law, appeared in the doorway, her hair in disarray, her white dupatta having slipped down from her head. Her bloodshot eyes bore into me like a laser, the anger in them sending a shiver up my spine.

"Now you come?" she asked. "You have any idea what happened here? They killed your brother. And you were not here to protect him, to protect us. They pounded him with hockey sticks, and iron rods . . . " She broke down.

Her two daughters, four and six years old, came running and wrapped themselves around her legs. I was still sitting beside Mother and couldn't find anything to say. The girls looked at me, their eyes full of fear. What unimaginable horrors they must have seen. I motioned to them to come to me. They clung to their mother, I reached out and pulled them gently toward me. They yielded without resisting and their little innocent bodies melted in my arms.

Father returned home with a few of our relatives. We embraced and he wept quietly. "So sorry I couldn't save Khalid. I just couldn't save him. They were so many and . . . "

"It's okay, Abba, it's okay. You could have done nothing," I said.

If it had been some tragic accident, he would have accepted it as cruel fate, the will of God. But this deliberate, premeditated lynching of his son was beyond imagination. Ours was not some barbaric tribal society where people lived in constant fear of one another, where it was normal to be torn apart by the feral rage of a rival clan. We had the rule of law and a common, basic trust in the decency of our fellow humans. How could such an atrocity have happened? How could it be *allowed* to happen?

Father said that if I had been present, they would have killed me too. Such was their fury. On Eid al-Adha, the family had slaughtered a goat, like they did every year. When Khalid went to the garbage dump to dispose of the animal waste, somebody had seen him and spread the canard that he had butchered a cow. In the evening, there were rumblings outside the house. Groups of men gathered on the street, shouting profanities, accusing us of killing the cow-mother. Aware of the lynchings of Muslims that had been taking place in other places, Khalid proposed to go out and clear any misunderstanding, to tell them that it was a goat they had sacrificed—that they could come inside the house and check the meat. But Father had stopped him. "Are you mad?" he said. "You think they will listen to reason? Let's sit quiet and hope they go away."

Khalid did not argue. He called the local police station and made a complaint. The police said they would look into it. Father knew this to be a mere formality and they would do nothing. The women in our house began praying and invoked the mercy of the Prophet and Allah.

The crowd thinned as darkness thickened, and everyone thought a tragedy had been averted. But Father said that the shouts and accusations had continued to ring in his head throughout the night. He had slept like a prisoner who would be hanged the next day.

The next morning, before the family could finish breakfast, there were unusual noises in the street. Father peeked out and noticed that a mob was gathering; in a matter of minutes, the crowd had swelled—mostly young men wielding sticks and pipes, hitting them on the ground, testing their weapons playfully. It felt as if the air had suddenly stopped moving. Khalid bolted the door from inside; Father helped him barricade it by moving the heavy chest-of-drawers against it. Then they all retreated into one of the interior rooms and locked the door behind them. Khalid kept frantically calling the police station from his mobile phone. Father called up relatives and friends, beseeching them for help, asking them to contact the police on their behalf—or the town's administration—or anyone who could come to their aid.

While they were still on the phone, the attack began. First came the rocks, and with them the abuse—You cut-ones, go to Pakistan! The chorus was loud and relentless. Then started the banging on the door. Soon they heard the hasp snapping, the wings of the door splintering, and the grunt of the heavy chest-of-drawers as it was pushed out of the way.

"We were all numb. The little girls began to cry," Father said. "They stormed into the house, started smashing things. Soon after, they broke into our room and attacked us. They slapped your mother. Razia took the girls to the corner and covered them with her body. They rained blows on her back. Then they dragged Khalid out on the street and pounced on him like wild animals. They kicked him and struck his head with pipes, with hockey sticks, blow after blow. I tried to stop them, but they had him surrounded on all sides. They kicked and slapped and pushed me away. I saw my son being beaten to death."

And he burst into tears. "Beta, I tried, I tried."

I accompanied Father to the police station to register a report. They denied having been warned. Father had recognized a few men among the mob. Some were from the neighbourhood and others from the street where his shop was. After some dilly-dallying, the officer noted down their names. A newspaper had reported that a local leader was the instigator. He had helped spread the rumour about the slaughter of a cow, aroused the mob, and spearheaded the attack. The police refused to make a note of his name. They asked for evidence. When I said it was their job to look for evidence, that I was merely quoting a news report, the officer told me to shut up and leave.

—

A week later, I was sitting outside on the steps of our veranda. Khalid's motorbike lay trashed in the corner like a hunted animal—seats slashed, lights smashed in, tyres ripped off from the rims, the spokes bent and broken—surrounded by a pool of motor oil.

Just then, two men opened our small iron gate with a clang and entered. Their skull caps and untrimmed beards made me wonder. I had not seen them before. They greeted me with elaborate salam alaikums and gave me a firm shake of the hand. The taller of the two said that they were from a Muslim organization whose name I could not catch. "What a tragedy," he said surveying the house behind me. "Please accept our condolences."

His companion, an intense young man with fireballs for eyes, added, "The kafirs have killed your brother. Are you going to do nothing?"

I looked at him impassively, not knowing what to say. He invited me to join their organization. "We meet every Friday. Come and see what we do."

I wanted to nod out of politeness but did not. Fireballs raised his foot on the step and leaned forward. He was chewing paan lustily, and the scent of sweet tobacco was on his breath. He patted me on my shoulder. "Silence in the face of atrocity is a sin," he said.

I lowered my gaze.

"They killed your brother. For nothing. Doesn't your blood boil?"

They said I should not feel alone and helpless; the men of faith were with me. The two prattled on in a glib, rehearsed way. They kept repeating that to suffer injustice silently was to sin against Allah. Before they left, Fireballs shook my hand vigorously and squeezed my shoulder as though jolting me awake.

"Your silence will not save you, brother," he said, before closing the gate behind him.

Saving Grace

At age ten, Salim's financial well-being was only partly dependent on the daily allowance he received from his father; the rest of it was due to means not strictly ethical. His father would leave some petty cash in his shirt pocket when he hung his shirt behind the door. When he was at his dinner downstairs in the kitchen, while Salim's mother waited on him, Salim would occasionally help himself to a rupee (or two) and a couple of quarters. Never more than that, he kept his greed in check. He spent some of this booty on kites, tops, marbles, and the sour candies he was addicted to. He saved what remained in his small piggy bank, which he carefully placed in the almirah with his clothes.

There was one problem in carrying out this heist. His father's shirt was out of Salim's reach. He had to jump, catch the collar, lift it off the hook at just the right moment, and land—all in one quick motion. He had perfected this act, but there was that one time when he had fumbled, and the collar had ripped. The mystery of the torn shirt never came to light. His mother blamed his father's carelessness, and his father puzzled over it, quite certain it was not his doing.

It was two weeks after Eid. Salim's grandfather had come visiting from Delhi, where in Chandni Chowk he had a shop of motor spare parts. Whenever Grandpa Hasan Ali was in town, Salim's finances received a boost. Grandpa doted on him, and Salim would use his charm to wheedle out a few coins from him.

Hasan Ali was a traditional patriarch, fair minded to a fault, a trait he said he had learned from the British who, despite all their faults were fair and just. His travels and life in a big city had given him a taste for good food and a smart getup. He carried a Swiss watch in the breast pocket of his jodhpuri jacket—its silver chain was always hanging out—and the wooden handle of his umbrella was inlaid with ivory.

Salim lived with his extended family of uncles, aunts, and cousins in a rambling brick house. At supper time, the women and children would sit around a large round platter and eat with their fingers. Men would be served later, after they had closed the shop, been to the "club"—where amid gossip and guffaws they played rummy or flush—and on the way back home stopped at the halwai for sweets and savouries and the bakery for rusk toast to accompany the next morning's tea.

One evening, Salim arrived late for supper, much to the disapproval of the women. Seeing the fare of khichadi and curd, he made a face and started his meal using a spoon he had taken from the kitchen rack.

"Hmm, since when have you become angrez?" an older aunt taunted.

Everyone used the same one spoon to pour the curd on their mounds of khichadi and also to drink it with. Sharing a spoon was not uncommon. Sometimes rice and curd (or some curry of the day) were mixed in the middle of the platter and everyone would eat from it.

"I have a cut finger, Chachi," said Salim.

"What happened?" Fatima, his mother asked, sounding a bit worried. All eyes focussed on the finger he held up.

"I cut it on the kite string."

"How many times have I told you to be careful?"

Everyone fell silent. But for the eating, there was no sound.

When supper was done, the platter, pots, and other utensils were piled up outside under a tree in the courtyard. By evening, the stack would have grown into a small unruly mountain. The area was curtained off from view with a bamboo screen. The cleaning lady, Sughra Bi, would come in later and wash in her characteristic slow, deliberate fashion. Old and thin as a reed, she looked at the world with dry, weary eyes; in her worn-out salwar-kameez, bleached of all colour, she blended unnoticed into the dark. Her good-for-nothing husband, an alcoholic, and her teenage lout of a son who had fallen into bad company lived off her meagre income.

Sughra Bi did not come in that evening, and it did not take long for the house to erupt into turmoil. The aunts cursed the woman, calling her lazy and irresponsible. It fell to Salim's mother and a younger aunt to do the dishes. The next day, Sughra Bi came, trembling with apologies. "I had an emergency, memsahib," she said to Fatima.

Fatima was upset, but mindful that Sughra Bi's other employers must have been laying into her all day, uttered a mild rebuke, "At least inform us when you are not coming."

"How?" asked Sughra Bi helplessly. She lived far and walked an hour each way to work.

The other aunt, however, smarting from the ignominy of having had to do menial work, lashed out.

Salim watched Sughra Bi receiving her scolding as he sat on the veranda doing his homework, a melon shake at hand. It seemed to have lost its taste. He never understood how his aunts, usually so loving, acted so cruelly toward the help.

When Grandpa awoke from his siesta, Fatima quickly came and poured him the shake. Grandpa made himself comfortable in the armchair, ready to sip his drink and read the newspaper. Noticing that Salim was staring into space, distracted from his homework, he asked, "Where is your mind wandering, young man?"

Salim snapped out of his reverie and smiled embarrassedly. "Dadu, why is Sughra Bi so poor?"

Hasan Ali folded the newspaper and became thoughtful for a moment.

"She has been unlucky."

"Unlucky! How?"

"She was unlucky to be born in a poor family. God created everyone equal, but that, as Ghalib has said, is a nice thought. In reality it doesn't work out that way, some of us are more equal than others. And this is the way it *is*." When Salim looked confused, Hasan Ali added, "Don't worry, beta. You'll get used to it. We all do, we all have."

Later, after she was done washing, Sughra Bi came to Hasan Ali and stood waiting with a request. Hasan Ali looked up and nodded.

"Saheb, I want a loan," mumbled the maid.

"Why?"

"My husband is ill in the hospital. His liver is bad."

"How much?"

Sughra Bi was quiet for a moment, as if making a mental calculation. "Six hundred."

Hasan Ali too was silent for a few moments, as though considering the preposterous demand. Then he said, keeping his tone polite, "You may not like it, but let me still tell you something. Your husband is a burden on you, a liability. He drinks all day. How much can a liver take? This was bound to happen. Don't bother with him."

"But he's my husband, Saheb."

"What kind of a husband is he? What has he done for you and your family? Your son is a loafer; he has taken after his father. Say I give you the money for his treatment and he recovers—then what? He goes back to his bottle?"

"But Saheb, I can't let him die."

"See, Sughra Bi, please try to understand. It's not that I don't want to help, but I don't see the point. Remember how I paid the fees for your son? I made sure that he had a chance to go to school, but he dropped out. God knows what he is up to now."

"My bad kismet, Saheb."

"You have to be strong. Don't give in to these useless men."

"He'll die, Saheb."

"Isn't he already dead to you? Why do you care?"

"Saheb, please."

"Sughra Bi, you know I'm not hard-hearted. But if I help you now, I'll only be prolonging your misery. I will not do that."

Sughra Bi stepped back quietly and left.

Salim had watched the entire conversation, and that night he could not sleep. What if Sughra Bi's husband died? He got up quietly, tiptoed to the almirah, took his cash box out and felt his way out to the veranda. Under the dim light of the porch, he counted the money. The notes and coins came to 40 rupees and 55 paisa—woefully short of the sum Sughra Bi needed.

The following day, when Sughra Bi was scrubbing utensils behind the screen in the courtyard, Salim ran up to her and handed her the fistful of his savings. She asked him what it was for, thinking his mother wanted her to run an errand. Salim shook his head. Realizing where the money came from, she refused to take it. But he pulled away and ran, leaving the money in her hands.

Before leaving for the day, Sughra Bi looked for Salim's mother to return the money to her. But Fatima was not home. Sughra Bi tied the notes and coins at the end of her dupatta and tucked the knot into the waistband of her salwar. At home, when she went to bed, she put her dupatta under her pillow. In the morning, when she reached for it, it was gone.

She knew who the thief was. She marched out, muttering curses, looking for her son Shakeel. She knew his haunt, which was at the end of the street. She found him and his buddies huddled up in an alcove hidden from the road.

Shakeel was around twenty, gangly, with small eyes and an angular face like his mother's, and a tangle of scruffy, strawlike hair. He was sitting on a cot, rolling a joint. There were two other boys with him, chatting and laughing. Seeing his mother, Shakeel closed his hand over the joint and signalled his friends to leave. Sughra Bi stood before him, panting. Shakeel sat still and looked her defiantly in the eye.

"Why are you here?" he asked in a hostile voice.

Without a word, Sughra Bi removed her plastic slipper from her foot and started raining blows on Shakeel's shoulders, face, and head. Shakeel grabbed her hand and pushed her away. "What is wrong with you, woman!" he shouted.

"What's wrong with *me*? You shameless bastard, you thief, give my money back. Now!"

"What money? What are you talking about?"

"What money? You good-for-nothing! That money belongs to a young boy. It's his savings—you understand—*his savings*. He gave it to me for your father's treatment. Shame on you, stealing a child's savings. Go drown yourself in a fistful of water. Give the money back."

"I don't have your money."

Sughra Bi started hitting him again.

"Give the money back or I'll kill you. I'll not allow you to spend a child's treasure on your filth. Where is it?"

"I don't have your money!" said Shakeel, pushing her away one more time.

She fell to the ground.

Two days later, at breakfast, Hasan Ali told Salim to get ready to go pick up a bicycle for him. Salim had waited long to own a bicycle. It was a hot summer day and Salim was in his usual shorts and shirt. His grandfather, on the other hand, as uncompromising as ever, wore a sherwani over pressed pants and a gold-threaded cap. Nothing else would do. As he walked he tapped his umbrella on the ground and swung it back and forth with a flourish. They stopped at a bicycle repair shop and picked a used bicycle. Salim simply nodded, without displaying the enthusiasm Hasan Ali had expected.

"What's wrong, beta? Aren't you happy with the bicycle?"

"I am," Salim said. Then haltingly, "Can I ask you something?"

"Go on."

Salim hesitated and looked around and asked his Grandpa to step outside. "Dadu, how much does the bike cost?"

"That should not concern you, beta. Just enjoy it. When you ride it, feel the thrill of owning your own bike."

"I want to know, Dadu. Please."

"Okay, if you must know, it's 350 rupees."

Salim started to speak, but couldn't get the words out. Hasan Ali pulled him close and patted him on his head.

"I don't want the bicycle, Dadu."

"Don't want it? Is it because it's not new? You're still learning to ride, so a second-hand would be good for you. You can knock it around. When you're an expert, I'll get you a brand new one."

"No, Dadu, it's not that."

"Then?"

"I want the money instead."

"Why? What do you need so much money for?"

"I want to give it to Sughra Bi," Salim blurted out.

"Sughra Bi?" Hasan Ali was puzzled. Then it dawned on him. "Oh, I see." He drew the boy closer and ruffled his hair. "Beta, it is very nice of you to think like that, but you should not get involved in the matters of elders."

"But Dadu . . . "

"Enough now, no more talk of this."

As the days passed Salim's initial inhibition faded. He began to use the bike for the smallest of things, even for an errand round the street corner. He would not step out of the house without it. On Sunday mornings he would clean it, wiping the rims, removing every speck of grime and dust from the frame, oiling the chain and the axle, and checking the brakes. When Hasan Ali left for Delhi, he promised to buy his grandson a new bike on his next visit in six months.

Sughra Bi arrived every evening to do her chores, pointedly avoiding Salim and his mother. She would disappear behind the screen at the washing place unnoticed, and when she was done, she would slink away quietly. Salim only hoped his money had brought some relief to her. He had no desire to know what she had done with it, and only wished that she would not tell his mother.

Finally one cold winter morning, Sughra Bi's son Shakeel came home to inform them that his mother would not be able to come to work that day. His father had died.

That evening, scrubbing the pile of dishes, the younger aunt grumbled and cursed Sughra Bi. The water was cold, and she had to heat it in iron pots over a wood fire. All that extra work incited further condemnation. But Fatima was moved and wondered aloud, "How did the poor woman use freezing water without a complaint?" The aunt said nothing.

The Passing Spring

The day my school principal caned me, because my hair was not cut short enough, my grandmother died. It was bright and warm, and we were a week into the school year. Our knapsacks were heavy with new books, all covered neatly and painstakingly in brown paper. Covering our text books and exercise books and writing our names, class, and the book's subject on the covers was a ritual invested with anticipation and foreboding. The smiles on our lips and the sparkles in our eyes were yet to be betrayed by the rigours of homework and the gratuitous meanness of our teachers. It was not as if we were not aware of the ordeals to come, but as children we lived in the moment.

And that day after the morning assembly came the first reckoning. As we were walking to our class in a single file, the principal tapped my shoulder with his bamboo cane. I stepped out. He reprimanded me for my *long* hair and whacked both my palms three times, after which he instructed me to get a proper haircut. What was proper depended on his mood. He was unpredictable and mercurial and therein lay his power to terrorize. To come home from school unscathed was no mean achievement.

Later that afternoon he sent for me; we were in the middle of our algebra lesson. I walked to his office, my palms curled from the morning torture, full of apprehension. Now what? I had been asked to pack my stuff and take my bag with me. Was I going to be suspended for my improper haircut? That would be a first.

I was surprised to see Uncle Mohsin in the office. So the suspension was official, I thought. Father was too upset and perhaps too ashamed to come himself, so he had sent Uncle to fetch me instead. As I appeared in the doorway, the principal looked up from his desk. "Your grandmother has died," he said. "Your uncle has come to take you home."

Grandmother dead? How? Why? My fear forgotten, I slowly stepped toward Uncle, not sure what to say or feel. He put his hand on my shoulder and squeezed it gently.

As we turned to leave, the principal said, "The haircut, remember!" My uncle looked at me, perplexed. I said nothing. As we walked home, he asked what the principal's warning had been about. I told him and he reacted with a grunt.

Grandmother, my nani, mother's mother was on my mind. Uncle Mohsin said that she had suffered a stroke, and before they could gather their wits and decide on a course of action, she had decided to leave the world.

For me and my sister, Nani had been a refuge from the troubles of the world—our small and cozy cocoon consisting of parents, school, and friends. Our academic life was Father's province. For him a good report card was the true measure of academic excellence, and fearing his wrath, we applied ourselves diligently to our studies. Everything else outside of books was under Mother's purview: how much we played, what movies we watched, who we made friends with. All mundane interactions required her approval. When we were unreasonable in our demands, she could be persuaded.

But on certain points of principle, she would not budge. The sticking issue with me was the matter of the sticky vegetables. Nothing got her goat more than my refusing to eat eggplants and okra. My sister Samina to my eternal incomprehension, relished them. On days when these vegetables were cooked for lunch, I would go hungry, and Mother would let me, without any compunction. Soon after, I would dash to Nani's house two streets down from ours. She would always have something available for me.

Nani's kitchen was on a terrace next to her bedroom. A round metal wire rack hung from the ceiling, out of reach from the mice and ants. In it she would store food and snacks. Refrigerators were still a novelty. The terrace was on the third floor and had a good view of the neighbourhood. I would come here many times to sulk, and stand looking down over the wall at the street below and brood over the particular injustice rankling me at the time.

Nani was frail and petite; she would have been around seventy. She coloured her hair black, unlike other women who used henna. No matter what time of the day or night I saw her, she was always dressed as if to go out, with not a strand of hair out of place. But she did not mind me and my sister appearing unkempt, with dirty hands and feet. Not so Mother, who insisted we wash up, because God alone knew what kind of dirt and germs we were bringing home.

Shunning meals was my favourite mode of dissent, but this had little effect on my mother. I found her indifference galling. Those afternoons, I would run to Nani's with swollen eyes and glum face, wearing the expression of a martyr. She would hug me and give me food and, for bonus, all the forbidden goodies—potato chips, sugar brittles, and slices of raw, sour mangoes. And when Mother happened to come by, she would be rebuked for her heartlessness. They would argue, and Mother would tell Nani not to interfere in her business, she was simply spoiling us.

And then their talk would smoothly switch to some totally unrelated topic; the argument about my welfare was forgotten and I would feel betrayed. I would listen spellbound at the nimbleness of their chit-chat as it shifted from topic to topic. When we parted, Nani would again admonish Mother, this time gently, telling her not to be so hard on the children. As we walked home, Mother would slap my back in mock anger and say, "Running to Nani like a mouse all the time."

Now Nani was no more. My nana had died many moons ago, when Mother was very young. I knew him only from the framed photo on the wall across from Nani's bed. As I walked with Uncle Mohsin that day I was comforted by the belief that Nani was surely destined for heaven and would be with Nana soon. When we reached her house a bunch of men in white skullcaps were standing outside in the street talking in low voices. Inside, in the open courtyard, Nani's body lay in a casket covered in a white shroud. Women sat around the casket on spreadout sheets of cloth, quietly weeping. I went straight to where Mother was sitting. "Your nani is gone, raja! Whom will you now run to, haan?" She burst into tears. My sister Samina was sitting beside her, and I took my place on the other side. With Mother's arms tightly wrapped around us, I too began to cry.

Two days later, Mother, Samina, and I were in our living room. Mother, wearing all black, was reciting the Quran in a low voice, I was doing homework, and Samina was listening to the radio, turned to a low volume. There was a knock on the door and Uncle Mohsin stepped inside.

Uncle Mohsin was Mother's cousin; Nani and his mother had been sisters. He was slight of build and so gentle of manner that people called him Allah's cow. He did not have a sister of his own and was very attached to my mother. On seeing him, Mother's eyes filled up. He came and took a place beside us on the floor. Hugging his leg, his chin on his knee, he sat staring at the floor without speaking.

Nani often said Mohsin was the sister Mother never had. Mother agreed, though she continued to be of the opinion that the love and understanding between two sisters just could not be replicated or substituted. She had three younger brothers, all of whom showered her with love and care. Still, for her, all their love, respect, and concern put together could never equal that of a sister. Men just did not have it in them, she would say, while sisters were truly made in heaven.

Uncle Mohsin too was made in heaven, in my estimation. He worked for Father as an accountant. He may have been polite but was not meek, and he did not approve of everything Father did. He flatly refused to cook the books when Father once asked him to find a loophole to skimp on taxes. "Everybody does it, Mohsin Saheb," Father had protested. "But I'm not everybody, Bhai Saheb," Uncle Mohsin responded. Father never broached the subject again.

Uncle Mohsin was meticulous in his work and his integrity could not be questioned. He would sit at his desk in the backroom of the shop, surrounded by shelves stacked with hard-bound ledgers. A lamp hung from the ceiling just above the table, shedding a sodium glow on everything. There was a table lamp handy, and a pedestal fan that he would use in the summer.

As a young boy, I had spent many an evening in that backroom, sitting facing him and reading comics or doodling on my sketchbook. Sometimes I would watch him closely and draw him. A picture of concentration—head bent, black-framed glasses resting on his aquiline nose, his bony fingers holding a fountain pen that moved steadily across the page. If Father happened to call him from the front, he would look up startled, as though from a trance.

All his movements were slow and deliberate; I had never seen him rush through any of his tasks. The way he walked, the way he raised his head to look at you, the way he put on his slippers, the way he sat down in the backroom of the shop and opened his fountain pen, there was an inner quiet, a contemplativeness, a steadfastness to his actions. Often this slowness irritated Father, who expected alacrity when he wanted to see something attended to.

Uncle Mohsin was not poor; he had inherited an ancestral home—a big haveli—which could fetch enough to feed the next seven generations. In Father's employment, he drew a handsome salary, but his wealth did not show on him. He always wore a white kurta-pajama, washed and neatly pressed. He never travelled; I can't think of a time when he was not in town.

His wife, Sharifa Aunty, a kind and unassuming woman, was cast in the same frugal mould. When I visited their home to play with my cousins, she would give us homemade sesame-seed brittles and chunks of dried coconut. During Ramzan, all my cousins would fast, and on Eid, their new clothes would be nice but sober and completely out of step with the current fashion. When the cousins got married, the ceremonies were sedate, the guests were few and the expenses modest. Instead of brash Hindi songs blaring from loudspeakers, there was a shehnai player—an old man, probably the last of the breed in town—who played soulful tunes all day long.

Uncle Mohsin was deeply saddened at Nani's death and was not shy of showing his emotion. As he sat with us in the living room, he quietly wept while Mother reminisced about Nani: how forthright she was with her opinions, had no malice in her heart, and was always kind. It was a wonder how she had managed to raise so many children on so little. Nani's travails were part of the family lore, and Uncle nodded in acknowledgement as Mother went through the list. He wiped his tears with a handkerchief and lifted his head to speak; his voice had the texture of rough cotton. "Who can understand the breaking of one's heart," he said. "Who can know the pain we carry. It's the things we don't see that are the heaviest."

I wouldn't understand the real import of Uncle Mohsin's words until twenty-three years later when Father died. His sudden passing left a vacuum not only in our lives but also, it would seem, in the physical environment around us. Father was a large man with a personality so imposing that in his presence you felt diminished. He was an art dealer and collector, a businessman with a passion that consumed his life. Our house was the extension of his character: big and expansive and furnished with art pieces and mementos and valuable, rare knickknacks. The fabric sofas were the refurbished heirloom from the rajas of Jaipur; the chandelier was also peerless, bought in an auction from the Nizam's palace in Hyderabad. The showcase almirah built into the wall displayed exotic curios from Mongolia, Ethiopia, and Palestine, as well as tribal artefacts from different parts of India. Unlike other homes in our community, the walls of our house were covered with paintings and photographs. Father took special pride in owning a couple of original Mondals and Pynes.

He had studied art history and anthropology in college, much to the chagrin of his parents, who predicted that he was setting himself up for failure and a life of penury. They didn't live long enough to be proven wrong. Hard work and luck had brought him success and he was always travelling, meeting important customers and seeking new specimens; his antique store was a gallery that drew tourists and aficionados. He specialized in objects created by uncelebrated craftsmen—he valued their utilitarian aesthetics, more so if they showed imperfections. He was enamoured of the Japanese concept called wabi-sabi, which was all about finding beauty in imperfect things. "Even God is not perfect," he would say. "Look at the world. Do you see perfection? Beauty, yes, but not perfection."

He became acquainted with this philosophy when, as a young man, he went to Kyoto on a college exchange programme to study traditional Japanese art. He fell so much in love with all things Japanese that his mother was relieved upon his return to see that he had not brought back a Japanese wife.

Father often reminisced about his days in Japan. He would joke that the person he fell in love with in Kyoto was not a woman but a man—a man long dead. Then he would chortle. The man was Basho, the seventeenth-century haiku master. He had brought back books of Basho's poems in translation. One of his prized possessions was a parchment scroll with a likeness of Basho sketched in clean spare strokes and one of his poems written in Japanese and English. He had the scroll mounted in a bamboo and glass frame and hung it under the wall clock. The juxtaposition was on purpose.

The passing spring
Birds mourn,
Fishes weep
With tearful eyes.

Time and its passing are interwoven into each other, he would often say, looking at the scroll. But at some point he must have fallen into taking time and its passing for granted. He had toured nearly half the world and acquired objects and tastes and a reputation which were at odds with our small-town mentality. Over time, our house began to look like a museum, and when money began to show in the decor, in the clothes we wore, and in the trips we took, people began to talk. Word went around that Father was a smuggler, a charge that amused and enraged him in equal measure.

But there was some truth to that public perception. Father would admit to an element of exploitation in his dealings with village artisans. But at least he brought their creations to the market, he would say. He wanted the world to appreciate not just the exquisite craft but also the people who created it. His transactions benefitted the artisans, who would otherwise languish in obscurity in far-flung villages and mofussils across our country. The business bettered their lives and at the same time continued the traditions, which without the financial incentives would simply die.

But Samina, the radical in our house, would not buy into his justification. She did not, however, have the nerve to argue with him. She was three years older than I and always had the itch to question everything. Mother called her a rebel without a cause; her hormones were going crazy, she would say. Samina went on to study philosophy in college and when she came home after the first semester, she grandly declared that God was dead. The idea found fertile ground in my mind. She went on to marry a lawyer, become a college lecturer, and have two daughters. Mother's joy then knew no bounds.

Samina now lived in Jaipur with her family and had come posthaste upon hearing of Father's death. I had flown down from Toronto, returning home after almost ten years. I was distraught and regretted being away from home and not seeing Father for such a long time. Samina was unreasonably apathetic. "To mourn a death is the height of arrogance," she said, "as if you and I are going to live forever." I told her there was a time and a place for philosophical explication, and this was not one. She smiled and gave me a gentle rap on my shoulder. "Acting all grown-up, haan!" She taunted. We were sitting in the living room with Mother and the scene was redolent of all those years ago when Nani had died. Just as then, Uncle Mohsin came to visit, and took his seat in the same place in the same posture. But twenty-three years had passed. He had become frail and everything about him was old; his skin, his face, his eyes. He smelt of soap.

Uncle Mohsin had stopped working for Father upon turning sixty-five, saying that he needed to devote his remaining years to the "upkeep of the soul." He was a widower now and had started spending his days at the small white mausoleum in our cemetery, tending to the graves of the revered divines of the community.

He was the first to arrive at the mausoleum every morning at six, and would immediately proceed with the cleaning; holding the long broom stick like an oar, he would sweep the courtyard with languid strokes, as though rowing a boat. Finishing with the courtyard, Uncle Mohsin would proceed to clean the interior of the mausoleum. Squatting down, he would pick up every speck of dust with a brush and pan and every fleck of flower petal. The red velvet on the three graves emitted a queer musty odour of sweat and rose at all times. Uncle Mohsin would remove the sheets and dust them before draping the graves again, fussing over every pleat, smoothing out every crease. When all the chores were done, he would go to the cistern at the other end of the courtyard and perform ablutions under a tap.

He would return to the shrine cleansed and pay obeisance—standing before each grave in turn, mumbling a verse and then bowing to touch his forehead on the velvet sheet. He remained by the graves for a long time. He would complete his obeisance by kissing the tomb three times, then walk to the mosque next door for the fajr prayers. He would then sit in the courtyard, lean against the wall and read the Quran.

Throughout the day, devotees came to pay their respects, among them his friends and acquaintances. Beyond the perfunctory greeting, nobody ever talked to him unless it was a matter relating to the maintenance of the mausoleum. At ten o'clock in the night, when the last of the devotees had departed and it was quiet again, except for the crickets chirping in the babul tree nearby, he would prostrate at the doorway facing the tombs, say a final prayer, lock the doors, and go home. Over the years, he had become a living, moving extension of the shrine. Not to see him around was a sign that all was not well with the world.

That day when he was visiting us on Father's death, there was something melancholic about him; he was like an ancient banyan tree that had seen too many winters. He exuded the simplicity, the earthiness of a man who has no artifices. He sat brooding, staring at the floor in his characteristic way, as though about to throw up timeless wisdom.

The sun was pouring through the windows, partly bathing Uncle Mohsin in its light. He listened quietly as Mother told him about the circumstance of Father's death, as she did to anyone who came or called to commiserate. Father had started his day as usual with a breakfast of three eggs—half-fried, always sunny-side up with runny yolk—and toast and tea. Then he had gone to the shop and returned home for lunch. He had eaten mutton curry, rice, and chapattis and licked his fingers with satisfaction; he always enjoyed his food. Normally he would go straight back to the shop, which was busy at this time of the year, and although his employees managed in his absence, he liked to attend personally to his customers. But that day he wanted to take a nap. He was tired. When she brought him his tea, he complained of a pain in the chest. She had made light of it, saying it was his usual acidity symptom. How careless of her, she now said. He said that this was different and described the shooting pain. Mother then called her brother. He came with an ambulance in no time and Father had been rushed to the hospital.

After a pause, she said that it was not the heart attack but the heartlessness of people that took his life. The ambulance was stuck in traffic and despite the siren and the driver shouting at people to make way, they just would not budge. How callous, how insensitive, she said tearfully, there was no decency left in the world. The doctor said that the patient had arrived fifteen minutes too late. *Fifteen minutes.* She stressed this like an incantation, her voice laced with regret and anger. He was only sixty-eight. This was not the age to die. But at least, she added by way of consolation, he had left the world quietly, with dignity, without much suffering.

Uncle Mohsin cast his eyes around the house; from where he sat, he had a good view of the living room, the kitchen on the left, and through the large windows, the front garden on the right. When Mother stopped talking, there was silence for a while. Uncle Mohsin's eyes were on the garden, following a sparrow flitting from bush to bush. After a while he looked at Mother and said, "What a life Bhai Saheb lived. Larger than life, just the way he was. Always busy, running here, flying there; buying this, selling that; art, properties, paintings." He paused, and his gaze returned to the garden. The bird had flown away. "All this for what? Now he is gone and all is left behind. Bhai Saheb had a great eye for beauty but . . . " There was remorse in Uncle's voice but also reproach. I waited for him to complete his thought, which he never did, staring out through the windows into the garden.

I glanced at Mother. She was staring at the carpet, perhaps trying to pick out the imperfections. Instinctively, my eyes wandered to Basho's sketch that Father had so cherished. *The passing spring.*

All Cut Up

1

Nobody talks to us. We have been declared infidels. We are officially excommunicated. Now friends don't call, relatives won't visit, and of course, nobody invites us over. All because I said no to an ancient, cruel practice that would have harmed my daughter. She is only seven.

My mother-in-law won't even look at me. She blames me for ruining her reputation, for bringing shame upon the family. I had never imagined that marriage would demand so much of me. During our courtship, Abizer and I had an understanding that I would continue to work after marriage. Abizer had agreed but he had not consulted his mother before committing. She had expected a compliant, obedient daughter-in-law who would bring her morning tea in bed, press her legs at night, welcome her many and frequent guests and cook meals for them.

Abizer and I were in the same college and happened to be taking the same class in history. He approached me once to borrow notes. This was an obvious ruse, but I humoured him because I found him cute. Tall and athletic, he had a friendly face and a shock of thick, black, curly hair. We started hanging out together, and soon developed an affinity that would eventually blossom into love and talk of marriage.

Being from the same community of Shia Muslims worked in our favour. The fact that my family was well-to-do and were loyal to the Syedna, the High Priest, further smoothed our path. We accepted Syedna's authority as we accepted gravity—as self-evident, God-given, and beyond dispute. My father paid regular tithe to him, no matter how much was demanded and how often. We never expressed a doubt or wondered what happened to all the money that was collected from the community. But at the same time, my parents kept their distance, unlike Abizer's mother, whose heart seemed to burn with an all-consuming fervour for the Syedna.

Abizer's father had died when Abizer was in his teens; since then his mother had dominated every aspect of his life, including the courses he took in college. He had kept our courtship well hidden. And so he had hesitated to tell his mother about me, afraid that she might reject me out of hand, for it was not up to him to choose his wife. He had found a job in Canada, and before he left, his mother insisted on finding a suitable match for him. It was only when she started looking around that he told her about me.

Her first impulse was to scold him. But then she made inquiries, from which she could glean nothing objectionable about me or my family. On the contrary, there was much that pleased her—our social status, our unblemished devotion to the Syedna, our flourishing business, and our house in an upscale locality. And so she agreed.

For the engagement ceremony, as was the custom, my family invited Abizer's family to our house. His mother had sharp features, and her thin lips did not admit an easy smile. She bore herself with exaggerated dignity in her prim and expensive lehnga-odhni, and behaved as though the world owed her respect. In our sitting room, looking at the portraits of the current Syedna and his deceased father that hung between two windows, she said to my mother, in a tone bordering on accusation, "Behn, don't you think the pictures should be bigger?"

My mother was not one to suffer a put-down quietly. "The frames are gold-plated, Sakina Behn," she said.

Abizer's mother nodded knowingly, and remarked that solid gold would have been more appropriate. Before my mother could react, Sakina Behn quickly changed the subject, to how she had the inside track to Syedna's family and was on first-name terms with the Behn Sahibas, the women of the household. She talked of inviting the Syedna, no less, to solemnize the marriage, and what an incredible honour it would be for us mortals.

During the days of our courtship, Abizer would sometimes mention that his mother was a strong personality. He spoke of her with great admiration. I had imagined that his idolization of her was like that of all Indian men, reared on the dictum that heaven resided at their mother's feet. Meeting her in person, I realized that there was a very thin line between respect and fear. She continued to control her grown-up children like marionettes, with subtle gestures—a slight flick of her finger to caution her daughter Arwa to sit properly and not cross her legs, an arched eyebrow to warn Abizer to tone down his over-familiarity with my parents. I was too swept up by the sense of occasion to be bothered by her overbearing manner. And later, before I had a chance to clear the air with Abizer, he left for Canada. In the two years he was there, we had long conversations on the phone. Once I reminded him of the incident with my mother regarding the photos on our wall and told him how rude his mother had been. He made light of the matter and asked me not to read too much into it.

Abizer flew down from Toronto to Mumbai for our wedding.

As promised by his mother, it was officiated by the Syedna and attended by members of his family and other grandees as well as some hangers-on. My father had given me a hefty envelope to be presented to the Syedna. He sat in a plush chair, and Abizer and I knelt before him with our palms joined, as before an idol. He offered me his hand, palm down, draped with a white handkerchief; I respectfully took it with both my hands and—as expected—slipped the envelope in his hand. I then proceeded to do the salaam—touching the back of his hand with my forehead, then both eyes, right and left, and finally with the lips. I kissed his knees, and then fell to his feet and kissed them too. Abizer did the same. Other members of our families were lined up behind us, clutching envelopes, giddy with nervous joy. I was not particularly enamoured of the Syedna, but meeting and touching him was an extraordinary experience. His hand felt soft and his handkerchief smelled of rose attar. The day before, my mother-in-law had visited our house, gathered everybody around, and instructed us on the protocol of engaging with the Syedna. She had modelled as the Syedna for me to practice with, and made me repeat the actions until I got them right.

On our wedding day, she strutted about like a prima donna, greeting guests with a thin-lipped smile and making sure that all procedures were followed exactly. When food was served in large platters to the entourage, she stood by, urging them to take more of the anjeer halwa and the shahi mutton roast and the saffron-infused biryani. Our nuptials seemed incidental to the larger spectacle orchestrated by her.

—

I came to Toronto in the summer, six months after our wedding. It was hotter than I had expected. On our way home I gazed out of the car window, curious to take in the city—the buildings, the people, the traffic. The cars kept to their lanes, and nobody honked. "Traffic is so quiet here, seems like a funeral procession," I said. "This is Canada!" Abizer said, beaming with pride. He then related an episode about an Indian truck-driver who had put up a "Horn Please" sign at the back, and the police arrested him for instigating drivers to honk. I smiled, only half believing him.

The first year of our life in Canada was the happiest. It was just the two of us, free to do what we wanted, no family obligations, no social pressure. I did not have a job for most of that year, so I spent all my time and energy into furnishing our home. We moved from our condo to a ranch-style house in the suburbs. It had a backyard which opened to a wooded ravine—a dream setting for someone like me, who had lived all her life in an apartment building. Our idyll was shattered, however, when my mother-in-law came to live with us.

She had been badgering Abizer to call her to Canada. His sister had married and moved to Dubai, and my mother-in-law was now alone in their big flat. Although she had a car and a chauffeur and a retinue of servants, she would rather be with us. She would miss the Mumbai life and her social circle, but she had heard great things about Toronto. Our community here, though small, was active and close. Her friends had apprised her of the local priest and his wife Behn Sahiba, with whom, it turned out, she already had a nodding acquaintance. I had no grounds to object to her coming. So Abizer applied for her immigration visa.

She arrived in Canada on a late summer afternoon when I was at work. I had taken up a job only the week before. That evening, when I returned home, a part of me was eager to see her; I was hoping the new place and the new atmosphere would soften her jagged disposition, make her a little more amiable. As I approached the house, there was a spring in my step.

But the moment I set my foot inside, I could feel a heaviness in the air. She was sitting on the couch and Abizer was across from her in an armchair. He gave me a weak smile and quickly averted his eyes. I put away my handbag and keys and went straight to her. I greeted her warmly, welcoming her to Canada. I reached for her hand to do the salaam, but she did not offer her hand, nor did she meet my eyes.

"What's wrong, Mummy?" I asked, confused, and looked at Abizer. He sat there like a condemned man—hands across his chest, head down, gazing at his feet.

"You cannot work," snapped my mother-in-law. "I'll not allow you to have a job." The attack was sudden and the charge unexpected. I turned to Abizer, who refused to lift his hangdog face toward me. And I felt betrayed.

For a moment I was caught tongue-tied. Then I regained my composure. "I'll work, Mummy," I said politely. "This was decided before marriage. You can ask your son." Not wanting to get into an argument, I quickly went upstairs to freshen up.

At dinner time, she sat at the head of the table with a swollen face and a stern look, talking to Abizer alone, asking him to pass the rice or the curry and finding fault with the food. The vegetable was bland, the chapattis were dry, was there no ghee in Canada? Before finally leaving the table, she mumbled, "Back home our servants eat better food." I ignored her. She was here to live with us for the rest of her life, and her tantrums—if today was anything to go by—would likely continue. I told myself not take her seriously about things I did not care about. And I did not care whether or not people liked my cooking.

When Abizer came to bed that night, I wanted to lash out. Instead, I turned my back to him and pretended to sleep. I knew he would want to talk. His breathing was heavy and I could feel his eyes upon me. I could picture him with his head propped up with one hand, the other ready to touch me gently on the arm. I squirmed on contact, pushed his hand away and told him not to touch me.

"I'm sorry," he said. "Never knew Mummy felt so strongly about you working."

I did not respond.

"Talk to me Zari, please," he said. "I know Mummy is being unreasonable."

I said nothing. His position was not enviable. He was beholden to his mother in ways I could not understand, but he needed to realize that now he had a wife toward whom he had obligations. His need to placate his mother I understood, but that need conflicted with how I wanted to live my life. He had not been transparent with his mother about me, and I did not want to let him off so easily.

"I'll choose to live the way I want," I said, turning to face him. "Within reason, of course." My tone was cold and matter-of-fact. "I respect Mummy but I'll not have her make decisions for me or my family." Abizer listened, his eyes on me, unblinking. His mother had harangued him already and now it was I. It was her first day in Canada and the house was already in upheaval. I did not want it to be this way. But I had to make it clear where I stood in this new family equation. Abizer pleaded for understanding. With time, he promised, Mummy would mellow.

It was a good thing that my job was a fait accompli when she arrived on the scene and she couldn't do much to dislodge me from it. Over time, she came to tolerate my having a career. An uneasy truce came to exist between us. I was always cordial toward her and let her have the reins of running the house. That gave her a degree of the power and control she craved. She decided the menu of the day and I cooked lunch before work and dinner after work. She planned the groceries and Abizer did the shopping. I gave her little opportunity for a confrontation, and that apparently irritated her. Without a reason to pick on me, she found it hard to assert her authority. But I was aware that behind my back, her grouses about me to her son continued.

I could have hated her, but for the most part I simply ignored her. I accepted her only because she was Abizer's mother. I did not want him to resent me for resenting his mother. I had his ear more than his mother did, and I too could have run a catalogue of grievances against her but that somehow seemed churlish. I wanted to keep our side of the relationship free of rancour.

Despite my restraint, my mother-in-law never had anything pleasant to say to me or about me. She did not help with the housekeeping, with the cleaning or washing. Menial work is not for me, she had declared. I did the cooking and laundry, and Abizer helped me tidy up the house on the weekends. She spent her days on the phone talking to friends and busying herself with social and religious visitations. Not before long, she began to host majlises, services in honour of the Syedna, to which her expanding circle of friends were invited. I refused to cook for them and asked her to have the food catered. She agreed to it only because she thought my cooking was no good and it would embarrass her to expose this fact to her friends. She insisted that I participate in the ceremonies. I did, but only for important occasions; from the rest, I excused myself. Every time I did not attend, we would have an argument, and inevitably my parents would be accused of not teaching me the requisite respect for our faith. I was a near-heretic in her eyes because I did not place the Syedna at the centre of my life. For her, the world began and ended with him. She hung his pictures in the hallway and in every room of the house. Every fatwa from high on was followed through with earnestness. Her ardour for the Syedna permeated our home the way the smell of Indian food did in others'.

—

When Zoya was born, my mother-in-law was satisfied, but not exactly thrilled. She would have preferred a boy.

"Tell your mother that *you* failed to supply the Y-chromosome," I said to Abizer.

"You don't expect her to know that, Zarina," he said.

"But she should," I replied. "I've been tolerating her nonsense all these years but this is the effing limit. And don't expect me to sit here and justify that girls are as good as boys." I paused to catch my breath and looked over at Zoya in her crib. "If it were in my power, I'd like to birth a girl every time. Just to spite people like her."

Abizer smiled. "All right," he said.

"I'm sorry, I didn't mean to snap at you," I said, feeling contrite. "I know you don't think like her . . . Zoya is as precious to you as to me."

Zoya was born after two miscarriages. Each time it happened, I hated myself. I hated my body for failing me. I felt robbed, incomplete, and incompetent. Those were dismal days. I missed home, I missed my mother. Abizer was very supportive, and his mother, though understanding of my condition the first time, did not take kindly to it the second time.

"You care more about your job than your family?" she rebuked. "Married for four years and nothing to show for it! Look at Alifiya, Sharifa's daughter. She's younger than you and has three healthy toddlers. Their house is bouncing with happiness. Know why? Because Alifiya's priority is her family and husband. If I had known you were such a stubborn woman, I would never have allowed you to become a noose around my son's neck."

It was a cold winter day and I had just come back from the hospital after the procedure. All I wanted was to be left alone; even on the ride home I had asked Abizer not to talk or make any attempt to cheer me up. His mother's voice felt like a screech of metal on glass. Something snapped.

"If there's any noose around here, it's you, okay!" I said.

"This is how you talk to your mother-in-law? Have your parents taught you no manners?" she yelled.

Abizer came hurriedly to me with a glass of water. "Please, calm down Zarina, you need to rest."

"Stop fussing over her, Abizer. It shames me to see you hanging on her skirt like this," scoffed his mother.

"Mummy, please drop it now," Abizer beseeched.

"What about dinner? Who's going to cook?" his mother demanded, abruptly changing the subject.

"Zarina can't cook. We can order out."

With a loud grunt and mumbling something incoherent, she left the room.

—

With Zoya around, the general cheer around the house improved. My mother-in-law became less ornery as time passed and actually began to take care of Zoya once I resumed work after my maternity leave. Soon after Zoya's first birthday, she began nagging us for a second child.

"The girl needs to play with a little brother," she kept saying. "It's time to have a boy."

I told her that the doctors had advised a gap of a few years between children, given my history of miscarriages, but somehow that never registered with her. This became another of her gripes, which she deployed as a barb when she needed to put me down.

2

The drive home from Toronto Pearson Airport was slow, the car crawling along in the Friday evening rush hour. Zoya, now seven, had been cranky through most of the flight and was now dozing in the backseat, exhausted. She did not want to come back to Canada.

We had been visiting my parents in Mumbai. In their apartment building in Andheri West, Zoya had hit it off with children of her age and hung out with them all day. She was curious, spontaneous, and eager to explore the new world she had come to, playing all day long with her new friends. She had eaten numerous ice-creams on the sly, against my strict order not to eat food from outside. Thankfully she did not fall ill. Some days I only got to see her at mealtimes and at night. In Canada I had often wondered, confined to suburban ennui and stifled by parental care, if she was missing out on a real childhood, and here, it was as if she was discovering play for the first time. On the plane, she grumbled repeatedly, "Canada is so boring."

Abizer had taken the morning off to pick us up. Shielding my eyes from the slanting rays of the late-August sun, I was thankful to be returning home, relieved to leave behind the chaos and squalor of Mumbai. Zoya would not agree, of course. I turned and looked over at her, her seat belt tight across her chest rising and falling with her breath, her eyes closed and head tilted to one side, fast asleep. Her face was calm, devoid of expression, and strands of loose hair streamed down her shoulders. Such innocence. I felt a tightness in my chest and tears rushed to my eyes, unbidden. I blinked and looked out the window.

"It's good to be back," I said airily, trying to cheer myself. A part of me was tense, and dreading what awaited me at home. Abizer looked across at me and smiled.

He knew what my mission in Mumbai had been. But it seemed

he had forgotten about it. Traditionally, most fathers in our community have little idea of what their daughters undergo when they turn seven. Their wives and mothers keep them out of it. It is considered the women's province. But I had told Abizer about it and about my plan to circumvent it. He had agreed, without showing much interest or trying to understand the significance of the issue. It was as though I were taking Zoya for a haircut. But with him in the know, I knew he would have my back. Women cannot fight their battles alone; we need men as allies.

No sooner had I entered our house than my mother-in-law asked, "How did it go?"

"All good," I said.

It had all begun when Zoya turned six. The morning after her birthday, my mother-in-law had told me that since Zoya was going to be seven the next year, it was time for her *khatna*.

I froze. I could not sleep that night. I had forgotten that all Dawoodi Bohra girls have to undergo circumcision, the ritual of female genital cutting. It had happened to me, and the memory of it still knotted up my stomach. There was no way I was going to subject my little girl to that mutilation.

But I could not bring myself to say this to her. Female circumcision is a custom sanctioned by tradition and mandated by the Syedna. My mother-in-law would rather die than disobey him. It was a sensitive matter, and I had no idea how I would get out of it. She kept reminding me of the rite every few weeks, and I would keep quiet. I did some quick research on the internet and was truly heartened to learn that female circumcision was banned in Canada, it was against the law. I silently thanked boring Canada for being on Zoya's side. I relayed the news to my mother-in-law, trying hard to conceal my glee. She said she had known that and was expecting me to get it done in India. My relief was short-lived.

But I thought up a scheme and let Abizer know. I took Zoya to Mumbai soon after her seventh birthday. The plan was to have a nice vacation and come back, pretending that the procedure had been duly completed. Mother-in-law would be none the wiser.

Two days after our arrival from Mumbai, it was a Sunday and I was in the kitchen making breakfast. The spring onions and green chillies were chopped and ready to be added to a bowl into which I had cracked five eggs. The frying pan was on the stove and I was about to add ghee to it, when I heard footsteps on the stairs. It was she.

I had been avoiding thinking about her. I said my salaams. She did not respond, and took her usual seat at the kitchen table. I felt anxious. Her stony silence and cold demeanour were clear harbingers of an impending storm. I poured a glass of warm water from the electric kettle, placed it before her, and stepped back to the counter.

"Zarina," she said. Her voice was sharp. "You and Zoya went to Mumbai for a purpose, yes?"

"Yes," I said, whisking the eggs, my back toward her.

"And that purpose was achieved?"

"Yes."

"You are lying!" she shrieked, banging the glass on the table, splattering water. A chill ran through my body.

"You are lying," she repeated.

I kept quiet.

"How dare you lie to me? I saw it."

"Saw what?" I spun around.

"Zoya. She is untouched."

A rage erupted in my belly. "You checked her? How dare you? Have you no shame?" I slammed the fork on the countertop and raced upstairs.

Mother-in-law had expected me to say sorry and grovel. My

reaction spurred her to greater vileness. She called out after me, shouting curses and questioning my upbringing, but I was quickly out of earshot and past caring. On the landing I met Abizer, who looked like a gosling frightened out of its nest.

"What happened?" he asked.

"If your mother so much as looks at Zoya again, I will scratch out her eyes."

"But what's the matter?"

"I'll not have that thing done to my daughter and you better tell her that."

"What thing . . . ?" he stammered, confused.

"You know what she did? She went and checked up on my little Zoya. How disgusting!"

Zoya was in the bathroom, brushing her teeth. I knelt down and wrapped her in my arms. "What happened, Ma?" she asked.

"Nothing, my darling, and nothing ever will." I smothered her with kisses.

—

The following day, when I returned from office after picking up Zoya from day-care, we had a guest in the living room—Behn Sahiba, the wife of our local priest. She was seated on the couch and my mother-in-law sat across from her on the floor. On seeing me, they fell silent. I greeted them with a salaam. I knew why she had come. I whispered to Zoya to go to her room and stay there until I came. I gave her an apple from the fridge, since this would be a long meeting.

"Come, Zarina behn, sit," Behn Sahiba said to me. Few knew her real name; they called her by her honorific. As the resident potentate, her husband treated the community as his fiefdom and was notorious for his short temper and acid tongue. Taking the cue from him, Behn Sahiba kept the womenfolk under her thumb, laying down rules and meting out punishment to those who flouted them. A small coterie of acolytes had sprung up around her, my mother-in-law being one of them. Wide of girth and short of height, in her colourful full-body hijab, Behn Sahiba looked like a potted plant flowering out of season.

I too sat on the floor. Behn Sahiba's position, as self-appointed dignitary, had to always be elevated relative to lesser mortals.

"You know who we are?" she began, forgoing pleasantries. "We are Mumins. The only Muslims whose faith is pure and pristine like the morning dew, untouched by the corruption of the world. We are the only ones on the right path, the path that leads straight to jannat, thanks to our infallible Maula holding our hand all the way. Under his mercy, we breathe, we live, and we prosper. Right?"

I nodded.

"And all this did not suddenly come to pass yesterday. A long thread of tradition from ancient times has brought us here. From generation to generation, customs have been handed down to us, and they carry the wisdom of our elders, of our Syednas. You do understand what I'm saying?"

I nodded, waiting for her to come to the point.

"These customs are for our benefit. They preserve our faith and our identity. They keep us on the straight and narrow. All this modern thinking—all this women's liberation—is not for us. Let the white women have them." She moved her weight and reached for a piece of barfi from the coffee table. Taking a bite and chewing, she continued, "For us, customs are compulsory. They are not a matter of choice. Religion is not a sweet shop from where you can pick and choose what you like. You do understand, no?"

I said nothing.

"Your daughter, what's her name?"

"Zoya," my mother-in-law mumbled. I clenched my fist, and

reminded myself to stay calm. If this woman threw religion at me, I would throw religion right back at her.

"Yes, Zoya. You know she has come of age. She must have her khatna done."

I waited for the words to sink in. "No, Behn Sahiba, I will not allow it," I said, and as soon as I said it, I felt unafraid. Ever since my mother-in-law had first broached the subject a year ago, I had decided that this practice would end with me; I wouldn't allow my daughter to be touched by it. I had done my research on the subject, read articles and blogs, scoured online forums and discussion boards, and written to Islamic scholars seeking their opinion. I knew this moment would come, and I was ready for it.

"Who are *you* to not allow it," Behn Sahiba raised her voice. "It is in our shariat. Our religion decrees it. It is good for our women. It keeps them chaste and out of harm."

"Show me where it is decreed in the Quran," I said.

"You are challenging me?" Behn Sahiba fumed. Accustomed to grown women genuflecting before her, being questioned by a nobody unsettled her smug self-regard.

"I want you to tell me where it is written," I continued. "Let me enlighten you. It is a North African custom. Our caliphs ruled that part of the world, and when people converted, they brought this social practice with them. There's nothing Islamic about it. Our scriptures written in the caliphs' times only reference it indirectly; it is not binding. And even if it were, I would not allow this barbaric procedure on my girl."

"So you are going to teach me religion now?" Behn Sahiba got up, clutching her patent-leather reticule, her heavy frame shaking under her flowery shroud. She turned toward my mother-in-law, who was also on her feet by now, palms joined, her face displaying a curious mixture of alarm and apology.

"What kind of evil sinner are you sheltering in your house?"

she asked her as she made for the door. My mother-in-law followed, begging forgiveness and beseeching her to stay.

"One more thing, Behn Sahiba," I said. I was emboldened, seeing her flee. "What you are advocating is female genital mutilation, which is illegal in Canada." I glanced quickly at my mother-in-law. "You people keep your hands off my daughter, or I'll report you to the police."

Behn Sahiba sputtered with rage. "Sakina Behn," she hissed, "You have a muddai, an infidel in your house. You are now an outcast. This family is excommunicated." She promulgated the fatwa and slammed the door behind her.

I ran upstairs to Zoya, triumphant and nervous. Excommunication is the equivalent of an attack dog; the clergy unleashes it to keep the herd in line. And it always works. The pull of the community, the need to belong, and the social pressure are usually so strong that I had seen the best and the boldest succumb to it, whimpering like lost puppies. Not me, I resolved.

But a dread settled in the pit of my stomach.

—

Following Behn Sahiba's fatwa, our family had become a social pariah. For me, it did not matter as much, because my interaction with the community was minimal and very formal. I would miss my friends, but some of them were quite open-minded and we could still meet clandestinely.

But for my mother-in-law, it was worse than death. The dishonour of being thrown out of the community—and especially from its inner circle—was unbearable. She had always counted herself among the chosen ones, the select few, and now she was shunned like a leper. The community was the sum total of her existence, giving purpose to her days and bringing repose to her nights.

Suddenly she had lost everything, and on top of that there was the shame and humiliation of it. Everybody now knew that her daughter-in-law was strong-headed and stubborn and that she had no control over her. For long known and respected as a tough, wilful woman, she had been shown up as weak and helpless.

She stopped talking to me. Through Abizer, our mediator, she demanded that I apologize to Behn Sahiba and that there were no two ways about circumcision, it would have to be done. I had him let her know that there would be no apology. I had done no wrong. It was Behn Sahiba who had been rude and called me names. As for the khatna, that day would never come, come what may.

Abizer agreed that an apology was out of the question but at the same time, was anguished to see his mother so crushed. She pestered him, invoking his manhood, to make me apologize. He left the matter to me. About the khatna, he did try to change my mind. In the days following the incident, his mother coached him on the importance of the rite, emphasizing that it was for women's ritual cleanliness and could even contribute to greater sexual enjoyment, that it was not a big deal, that I was making a mountain out of a molehill.

One evening I was reading in bed when Abizer approached me directly. He took my hand and looked at me, his eyes pleading. "Why are you making such a fuss?" he asked, and rattled off the virtues of the khatna he had learned from his mother. "It's only a nick, after all. We men also get circumcised, do we complain?"

"It's not just a bloody nick," I shot back, closing the book. I pulled my hand away and drew the comforter tighter around my shoulders. "It's not the same as what they do to you. Medically, it is beneficial for you guys; there's research to back that up. But for us girls it is downright harmful, cruel, and unnecessary; it compromises our sexuality, causes lifelong mental trauma. When boys are circumcised, there is a big celebration. You remember yours, don't you? People bringing you those boxes of cracker biscuits? Why cracker biscuits, for heaven's sake? Is that what boys crave when their willies are snipped?"

Abizer seemed amused by the imagery.

"For the girls, it is done in secret. It is a hush-hush thing, as if it were a crime, which of course it is. It is a bloody crime, an assault on their innocence. You know the nights when I say I've a headache and you turn away in frustration? You probably wonder why I'm so frigid. I'll tell you today—I don't enjoy sex. I force myself to do it, for you."

Abizer sat up, his interest suddenly piqued. He stroked the back of my hand. "Don't tell me it is because of your khatna?"

"It is," I said, my body tensing, an ache shooting up my neck. "It has scarred me. I don't think I've ever told you how it happened with me, have I?

"I will never forget that day. I was in the third standard. School had just closed for the summer, and Mumbai was being lashed with monsoon rains. One morning, my mother told me that tomorrow we were going to Matheran. Let's go and say goodbye to Nani first, she suggested. I was overjoyed at the idea of a holiday at the hill resort. I wore my pink and blue frock, and we walked down to Nani's flat a block away, avoiding the puddles and potholes.

"Nani hugged me as soon as I stepped inside. There was an old woman at her place. She had white hair and her two front teeth were missing. When she smiled at me, the tip of her tongue stuck out through the gap. She spread a bedsheet on the floor and asked me to lie down. 'Yes sweetie, lie down,' said my mother reassuringly. Although it was an odd request, especially in the presence of a stranger, I lay down without thinking much of it. At age seven, I would have done anything my mother told me to. There was Nani there, too, so what was there to fear, I thought.

"The woman took out a flat tin box, the kind in which English toffees came. She squatted on her hams beside me and opened the box. Its purple design was fading, and I could not see its contents. Nani pulled up my frock and removed my panties, then made me stretch my legs wide and pinned them down. My hands were on my chest, and mother held them tight. I was confused, not sure what was happening. I looked at Nani and then at Mother over my head but neither of them was looking at me.

"Suddenly, Mother said, pointing to the ceiling, 'Look, look, birdies.' There were no birds. As I wondered what had got into her, I felt a sharp, stinging pain down there. I gave out a cry. Mother said, 'Look, look, birdies flew away.' The woman pressed down a piece of cloth between my legs. There was a burning sensation. I yelped in pain and started crying. The woman gave me a sweet. Then I saw blood. I cried more, still not sure what had happened, and still too scared, too confused to find out.

"For two days, it hurt when I peed. Then it stopped hurting. But deep inside, the wound never healed. We never went to Matheran. I was heartbroken. Whatever they had done, they had broken my trust, Mother and Nani. I lost more than my clitoral hood that day. Whenever I recall the incident, it is not the physical pain that I remember. What stings is the trauma, the memory of that violence, the breaking of trust. These are the things which haunt and hurt even now. That's why I recoil when you touch me there. It fills me with dread. The body remembers. Each time, I'm scared as if I'm going to be violated again."

Abizer was quiet. "Didn't you talk to your mother about it?" he asked after a few moments.

"I did," I said. "Many years later, when I was in college. She was reluctant to discuss it. Said it was the custom, the option of not doing it was never there. But she was wrong. There is always an option. I've created one for our Zoya. And please know, it has never been just a bloody nick."

Boys Will Be Boys

Mo and his gang had a thing about dogs. They instinctively reached for stones the moment they saw one. They would attack the mongrel with savage glee, as if not to hurl a rock would be to violate some secret, adolescent covenant. And no schoolgirl ever escaped their catcalls. When girls saw the gang approaching, they turned around and changed their path. Clueless village yokels got their turbans tossed and dhotis pulled. The gang would steal coins from unsuspecting beggars and then descend on a shop—all seven of them—yelling and jostling, pestering the shopkeeper to show them this or that from behind the counter. When his back was turned, they would have a go at the jars on the countertop, pocketing cookies and lozenges and anything else they could get their hands on.

Mo was my older cousin, and such were he and his friends. They must have been in their midteens, oozing testosterone and tumescent with more energy than our small town had the wherewithal to channel. People wondered what their mothers had eaten before bringing them into the world. Somehow they had escaped the petty-bourgeois pieties and pruderies of their middle-class homes. Singly, they were decent fellows whom a mother might willingly consider for her daughter. But when they came together, they morphed into a different beast altogether, bringing constant complaints and shame to their parents, and one which respectable people kept their distance from.

I must have been eleven or twelve at the time and had no friends my age, and so sometimes I hung out with Mo and his crew. I was in awe of the whole rowdy lot. Their treatment of young boys was only marginally better than that of dogs. But I was spared, for nobody dared to mess with Mo's kid brother.

Hashim was Mo's only challenger. Tall and strapping, he hated Mo's guts and made no secret of it. The two would often get into arguments and end up on the ground in a knot. The rest of the crew would watch in amused indifference, inciting the one who was on top to sock it to the other. There was no loyalty or sense of right or wrong. Having fun was the end, and the means to achieve it was mostly foul.

This was no more evident than in the case of Mulla Tahir. In the small courtyard of his mud house, Mulla Tahir ran a madrassa for children. Lanky of build, gaunt of face, and rheumy of eyes, in his faded sherwani and pajama and round skullcap askew on a balding head he cut a sorry figure. He was a strange amalgam of contrasting attributes—funny and tragic, fearless and timid—and inspired neither fear nor respect. He had a brood of daughters to feed and struggled to make ends meet. For extra income, Mulla Tahir volunteered to act as witness to marriages. Mulla Tahir bore witness to every nikah in town—and had been doing it since time immemorial, it would seem. With his toothy smile and a sardonic curl at the corner of his mouth, he was seen in the wedding albums of at least two generations.

Mo and the gang toyed with Mulla Tahir the way cats would with mice, tormenting him with the kind of wickedness only their species was capable of. When he was out in the street, they would sidle up behind him and pull the hem of his coat, then scoot away. Irritated, he would turn around and let loose a volley of vile abuse; onlookers would laugh. When Mulla Tahir wrote on the blackboard during class, they would hurl missiles of crumpled paper and pieces of chalk at him and break into giggles whenever he turned around and launched a tirade.

In my boyish innocence, I admired their audacity. I thought they were a cool bunch, brassy and unafraid. They went looking for rules so they could break them. One day the gang happened to be at the community hall for a meal. They always arrived at such events with voracious appetites and stuffed themselves until the pots in the communal kitchen were upended by the servers. The meal was served on a large platter, around which they sat in groups to eat. That particular occasion was teeja, the third day of mourning for someone. Mulla Tahir had staggered in late that day and having nowhere to sit ended up joining the gang. When the food arrived, Mulla Tahir shut his eyes to say the fatiha, the customary prayer for the dead, recited over a sweet dish at the beginning of a meal. When he had finished and reached for the sweet dish, it was empty. The poor man almost looked skyward to see if the halva had flown away. The gang cackled brazenly. To protest would have simply invited more ridicule. Meekly, Mulla Tahir swallowed his loss and remained vigilant for the rest of the meal.

Street donkeys were also a source of amusement. There was always an odd one, sickly and abandoned, wandering about. One morning the gang waylaid one such unfortunate creature while it was nuzzling a broken drainpipe. Mo lassoed it and took it home, tethering it outside the compound gate. He asked the boys to feed him a bunch of straw and gave him a drink of water. Satiated, the creature accepted the new master and was ready to do his bidding.

For what purpose Mo had taken in the donkey, nobody knew. "He's my pet, his name is Genius," he declared. Daily, the gang would take Genius for a walk through the streets. Everyone took turns holding the rope around his neck, as though Genius were a prized thoroughbred deserving of the world's attention. Invariably, one of them would sit astride Genius and try riding him like a horse.

One evening, while thus loafing about, the gang crossed paths with a female donkey. Genius snorted, brayed softly and stopped, refusing to budge. In no time, his member came into self-awareness and made its presence felt. The gang was in splits. Sabir, always the prankster, kicked Genius in the butt. Mo nudged me and winked, and I looked on, aghast.

"Naughty fellow is ready for action," he said. "And I've found my mission. We have to get that female."

"What for?" Sabir asked. Mo ignored him.

The female was not a stray; she belonged to a dhobi.

Mo approached the washerman and asked, "Is this donkey yours?"

"Yes," the washerman replied.

"You see that donkey over there? He's mine."

"Okay. You also a dhobi?"

"Nooooo," Mo exclaimed loudly, affronted. Then he whispered, "He has a problem."

"What?" The washerman gave Genius the once-over. "He looks weak. Give him something to eat."

"No, the matter is a little delicate. You see, he is in love with your donkey."

"What nonsense? How can you tell?"

"Well, see it for yourself."

"Oh, that. He's just horny, not in love."

"Well, I was being polite. I'm from a respectable home."

"Okay, okay, what do you want me to do?"

"No, no, not you," Mo mumbled, stifling his laughter, looking at his crew. "It's your donkey we want. Can we borrow her for a couple of hours?"

"What? Get out of here? Who do you think she is? A whore? She is also from a respectable home."

"Of course," Mo said, smiling, and thought for a bit. "Okay, let's do it the proper way."

"What do you mean?"

"Look at Genius, how handsome he is. All he needs is some action from time to time, just like you"—Mo giggled—"I mean, like all of us. If not, he goes mad. Like a donkey, you know."

"I told you, my Anarkali is a decent girl. She's not here to satisfy random geniuses," the washerman said.

"Anarkali! That's a beautiful name for a beautiful filly." Mo was enthused. He put his arm around the washerman's shoulder in an attempt to befriend him, and asked him his name. Sukhram, the man said, backing away. Mo leaned into his ear and whispered, "Sukhramji, let us make it proper." Then, more loudly for the benefit of his audience, "I'm thinking of marriage. Let me formally ask for your Anarkali's leg for my Genius."

Sukhram began to walk away. "Fuck off."

"I'm serious Sukhramji."

"You take me for a fool?"

Mo kept pace with him, pulling Genius behind him. "Wait Sukhramji, I mean it."

Sukhram stopped.

"I want my Genius to marry your Anarkali."

Sukhram considered the offer, wondering if this fellow was pulling his leg. "That's all fine, but Anarkali will have to go to her husband's house after marriage. I cannot allow that."

"Hmm that's a problem," Mo said, and was quiet for a few seconds. "Okay, as it turns out, our Genius is quite progressive and wouldn't mind living in his wife's home."

"Okay, works for me."

"There's another thing."

"What?"

"Dowry. I'm giving you my well-bred Genius. His upbringing has cost me a lot."

The washerman was again lost in thought. "Dowry is illegal, you know."

"Not for donkeys."

"Okay, how much?"

"Five hundred."

"Fuck off."

"You will have an extra two pairs of legs to work for you. And he's a good stud who will sire a new generation of geniuses. It's not a bad deal."

"Fuck off."

"Okay, how about 300?"

When Mo had quoted 500, we had all gasped. The poor washerman might not be earning that kind of money in a whole year. Even 300 rupees seemed like an astronomical sum. But Mo was nothing if not bold. So they haggled. Mo climbed a notch down with every new offer and each time he was told to fuck off. Finally, the dowry was settled at 50 rupees.

Then there was the question of how the marriage should be solemnized. Mo insisted that Genius was a Muslim and that a nikah was in order. Anarkali would have to be converted.

Sukhram balked at the suggestion. He sighed and shook his head wearily, perhaps wondering what an asinine drama he had got himself into. "Mister, stop wasting my time. This is not going to work."

"Why?"

"This Hindu-Muslim thing. Giving away a Hindu female to a Muslim male is a very bad idea. It is love jihad; you know that, don't you? As it is, you're seducing and converting our girls. Now you're after our donkeys too. If they come to know of this, they will kill both."

Mo's smirk vanished. He had not expected his silly little game to get embroiled in politics.

"If you want this done," Sukhram continued, "it will be according to Hindu rites. Take it or leave it."

"Okay, whatever you say," Mo said.

"No, Mo, that's not right," Sabir interjected. "We cannot marry off our boy to a kafir. This is haram."

A few others nodded in agreement. Mo looked at them in surprise, wondering when this shameless bunch had started caring about religion. "You're not joking, right?"

"Religion is a joke to you?" Sabir was angry.

"Well, in that case, Genius is mine, and I'll decide who and how he marries," Mo said sternly, patting the ass on the head and lovingly rubbing the side of his neck. Turning to Sukhram, he added, "We'll do it the Hindu way."

Sukhram led the entourage to a nearby temple. He bought two marigold garlands from a flower-seller and gave one to Mo. Each proceeded to help their animal with the ritual of exchanging garlands. Sukhram then demanded that a fire be lit. Mo signalled to us; we went around looking for twigs and pieces of wood and made a fire in front of the temple. Hashim tended to the fire. Sabir had refused to join the ceremony.

As the fire got going, passersby paused, and idlers and stragglers from around the neighbourhood gathered. Sukhram motioned the crowd to spread out. He extended the length of rope from Anarkali's neck and tied it to Genius's leash. Then he asked

Mo to lead Genius around the fire and he followed with Anarkali. Someone in the crowd started singing a popular bhajan and others joined him.

When they had walked around the fire seven times, Sukhram announced that the animals were now husband and wife. Hoots and cheers rent the air, and people began banging pots and pans. A sweetmeat-seller nearby brought over a box of gulab jamuns and presented it to the wedding party. Before our crew could swoop on it, Mo gave one piece to Sukhram who had started to walk away with the two donkeys.

Mo said, "Not so soon, Sukhramji. Where's the dowry?"

Sukhram, smiling apologetically, reached into the vest under his shirt and retrieved a small roll of notes. He counted out five ten-rupee notes. Mo patted Genius. "Be a good boy, and better go easy on your wife. Okay?" Sniggers went up.

With fifty rupees in his pocket, Mo swaggered like he had won a lottery. It was understood that the money was not just for Mo to keep. It belonged to the gang and was to be spent on their collective enjoyment. But how? Everyone had an idea, disagreement was rife, and they soon came to blows. In the end, Mo settled on a camping trip to a small farm in a nearby village.

And so on a Saturday afternoon, we found ourselves outside our house with gunny bags filled with pots and pans, groceries, and other necessities strapped to the sides and racks of our bicycles. The party made quite a production, shouting and yelling at each other and blocking the street. People had to pick their way past us. Sabir, who had boycotted the wedding on doctrinal grounds, had no qualms in joining the celebration, the first to arrive and making the most noise.

It was late afternoon by the time the convoy got going, watched by the neighbours. The boys rode ahead in twos, shouting and frolicking about, letting the world know of their expedition. Mo was last, with me on the crossbar. Our progress was slow, and it got dark before we reached the farm. The full moon illuminated our path, but on the sides of the road the darkness was like a wall. The boys made creepy noises to spook each other.

Upon reaching the farm, we set up camp in the open under the starry sky. The moon had inched eastward and now shone coyly behind a lone cloud. I lay down on a cot while the boys played cards by the light of an oil lantern. The night buzzed with crickets, their crik-crik overlaid with the strange sounds of other nocturnal creatures. The smell of manure was thick in the air; cows mooed in a nearby barn. A dog's bark reached us like a lament from a distance. Hashim said dogs cried in the night when they saw ghosts. I scrunched up in fear, pulled the sheet over my head and wondered if it had been a good idea to have come at all.

When I awoke, the boys were slurping tea and dipping toast in their cups. "Somebody prepare breakfast for the prince!" Sabir taunted. In the soft slanting rays of the sun, the farm looked like a dream vista. Across the field, I could see a farmer's hut, the well with its mandatory waterwheel, the velvet green shoots of a young crop. I was curious. "What are they growing?"

"Grass for donkeys. Would you like some?" Hashim said with a chuckle, looking around for approval.

"Hey, leave the boy alone!" snapped Mo.

I got up and splashed my face with water from a bucket and realized that I had not brought my toothbrush. I called out to Mo, "I forgot my brush."

"You also forgot your mummy," Hashim said, and this time everyone laughed.

Mo said they had all chewed a neem twig. Would I like to do that? I nodded and he threw one to me. The twig was bitter but I did not complain for fear of being laughed at again.

Later in the morning, Hashim came running, holding a chicken by its legs. It was making a racket and flapping its wings. Hashim was as excited as the bird was terrified.

"Dogs were harassing the poor thing. I rescued it," he panted, proudly holding it aloft.

At the prospect of chicken curry, a wave of thrill swept over the campers. Everyone had suggestions about where to slaughter it, for it could not be done openly. It was a Hindu village and eating meat or killing animals was sacrilegious. We had learned to be discreet about these things from a young age. But Hashim was too excited to care and went ahead and butchered the fowl behind a temple. Mo was pottering around the farm and when he learned what Hashim had done, he was livid. "If they find out, they will slit our throats!" he screamed. "It's like them cutting a pig in front of a mosque."

"Oh please, scruples don't look good on you," Hashim retorted. "These village idiots don't have a clue. Nobody will know." He was kindling a fire in a makeshift brazier while brushing the smoke from his eyes. "By the way, you're having none of that chicken."

Mo lunged at him like a bull but the others grabbed him. "Idiot, you know we can't mess with religious shit," he said furiously, shaking himself loose.

The fracas was forgotten when it was time to eat. Mo relished the curry, licked his fingers and complimented Sabir, who had cooked. Hashim needled him over his outburst. Mo spat out a piece of gristle and said nothing.

In the afternoon, as we lazed and chatted in post-lunch torpor, Hashim alerted us to the presence of the opposite sex in the vicinity. A sudden hush fell over the camp and everyone strained to listen. Female voices, thin and sharp and sweet, wafted through the gauzy heat enveloping the village. A surveillance party was quickly dispatched. It reported that the visitors were indeed of the female variety and added, to everyone's delight, that they were of familiar vintage. Another wave of thrill passed over the gang.

"From chicken to chicks," Sabir grinned. "We're in luck today."

"Let's go," Mo said, stubbing a bidi under his flip-flop. He motioned to me and I padded along with a couple of others in tow.

The girls were playing cards in the veranda of a two-room bungalow that had seen better days. They sat in a circle on a neatly laid-out calico bedsheet; their slippers stood guard behind them. Rashida, who lived on our street, saw us coming and said something softly, nodding in our direction. Heads turned in unison, and a few groaned in open disapproval.

"Hello," Mo launched his gambit. "Can I also play?"

There were a few chuckles.

"I have an extra joker," he said, pointing to me.

They all laughed. I kicked Mo in the shin, stung by the insult.

"Your joker is too young . . . for us," one girl said.

Mo was pleased by the suggestive response. "Take me, then," he said. He winked at me, and I kicked him again.

The girls squirmed. The rest of the gang had caught up with us by now, and we stood around them, reeking of sweat and dust, the smell of curry on our breaths. "Guys, we need air," complained one of the girls, wrinkling her nose.

"Hello, allow Queen Victoria to breathe," Hashim said.

Mo, who was standing behind Rashida, soon seated himself on his haunches and started kibitzing her on strategy.

"Mind your own business," she said, half-mockingly.

"If you get rid of this one," he persisted, pointing, "by your next turn you can declare rummy."

The girls howled in protest. "Keep your snotty nose out of it," Queen Victoria said.

Mo laughed, unfazed. Though I was still seething at his betrayal, I couldn't help marvelling at his felicity with the girls. In their presence, he was a different person. Absent was the smartass bravado; he was funny and charming instead, a naughty smile flitting on his lips as he parried their insults with endearments, only to elicit more jibes.

Rashida followed his advice and won. The rest of the group erupted in protest, called Mo names and told him to go make himself useful elsewhere. The girls then began another round, ignoring the boys, hoping that they would get bored and leave. But the boys were like bees around flowers. They buzzed around, bantering and teasing the girls, picking on the styles of their hair or the colours of their scarves; the bold ones badgered some of them to hook up with them after school. Unable to concentrate, the girls gave up the game half way. Somebody suggested that it was time for tea.

"Yeah, good idea," Sabir blurted out. "We boys have the tea; you girls bring your milk."

The gang snickered as the girls frowned, their faces flushed. I was too young to understand the import of what was said, but I knew that something nasty had been uttered.

Seeing Rashida pumping the kerosene stove, Mo went over to give her a hand. They whispered as they got the stove going. Somebody fetched water from the well and poured it into a large saucepan. As it started to boil, cups were brought out and snack packets were opened. When the tea was ready, Rashida and Mo ambled off into the field with their cups. Sabir called rudely after them. Mo swung back and flipped him the finger.

Queen Victoria came over to me as I sat reclining against a pillar and asked what I was doing with such louts. They are my friends, I proudly corrected her. She laughed.

"What's so funny?"

"You can do better," she said and walked away, ruffling my hair. Then she turned back and winked. For days, that wink stayed with me.

When the girls started packing up, the boys sprinted to our campsite and began gathering stuff with a furious urgency in order to accompany the girls on the way back.

While loading a bag on his bike Mo noticed that the rear tyre had been slashed. He checked the front tyre; it too had been ripped, and the inner tube was spilling out. The boys cursed the mothers and sisters of the perpetrators as they discovered how tyre after tyre had been slashed.

"Motherf . . . !" shrieked Hashim.

"This is all your fault, you idiot," said Mo through gritted teeth.

Hashim punched him in the face, and in no time the two were rolling in the dust. The rest paid them no attention as they tried to make sense of what had happened.

"They've butchered them, don't think they can be repaired," said Sabir. "We'll need new tyres and tubes."

The girls had long departed, and were forgotten. We began a slow trek home, dragging the bikes along. The mood was sullen, as if retreating from a battle, defeated. If anyone spoke, it was only to utter profanities.

Joint Venture

Ruchika and I had an easy, backslapping friendship. She was a good sport, with a sense of humour with a caustic edge to it. And it often seemed as if that edge was reserved for me. In college, we used to spar and argue with each other as much as we, as a team, did with others. We would take part in debate competitions and always choose to speak, just for kicks, for the "wrong" side of the motion. We had founded the Patriotic Scoundrel club and would lampoon all the sacred cows of the day. During the national Emergency under Indira Gandhi our club drew irreverent cartoons of her and plastered them on the college walls. That didn't go down well with the guardians of the state and we nearly got suspended. Anyone who was pompous and pretentious got a taste of our indignation. There was a rich popinjay who strutted about like he owned the college; a bunch of acolytes followed him around. Now and then we punctured his motorbike and enjoyed seeing him hopping mad.

Ruchika used to smoke openly, scandalizing professors and students alike. New students would stand and stare at her, mouths hanging open. Her sense of joy, her intrepid nature, and above all, her eagerness to show the finger to the puritanical types had made her dangerously attractive—to guys like me who fantasized about breaking rules and smashing conventions. People often mistook us for an item. I wouldn't say I wasn't romantically inclined toward her. But the feeling was ambiguous. Ruchika was attractive but not in the conventional way of being fair and cute and all that. Of average height, she had a round, pleasant face and big lucent eyes. Her skin was the shade of burnt sienna and she had a shapely figure which, as far as I knew, had never donned traditional clothes. I had always seen her in pants and tops. Her permanent pixie cut seemed like a protest against long hair. She packed the energy of ten people and a horse, and could be quite a handful sometimes. She was a fun companion but also a firecracker. We were open and candid with each other on many things but, oddly enough, we never addressed the softer side of our relationship.

We visited each other's homes often. Our families, middle-class and mostly progressive, seemed to be fine with a boy-girl friendship, which in other social circles would have likely raised eyebrows. Ruchika also had the habit of touching me, tapping on my arm to make a point, holding my hand in a crowded place, massaging my shoulders now and then if I said I was tired. I tried to read into every touch and gesture, but all I found was a casual, unselfconscious, no-big-deal kind of attitude. There was no guile, no agenda, no leading on.

I had hoped, despite the reservations I had about her free-spiritedness, that she would come to see me as more than a friend. I bided my time. Then one time we happened to be talking about our careers and what we wanted to do with our lives and that sort of thing. I remember mentioning that I wished to go into civil service. She looked at me with surprise and laughed. "You are a patriotic scoundrel, after all," she taunted. She wanted to go abroad, she said. India was no place for people like her, it was too suffocating. "The society bears down on you like oppressive heat," she said, wiping sweat from her upper lip. "One can't be oneself here."

I asked her what she meant by that. She appeared to consider the question for a long moment and then she said I would not understand. It was not in her nature to be reticent, so I wondered what was holding her back. It felt like rejection. Suddenly I was not worthy of her confidence. That and her desire to go abroad created a chasm between us. We wanted different things out of life. Some corner of my heart constricted, and it was clear that any romantic notion I may have had would have to be put away.

One spring afternoon, not long after our postgraduate exams Ruchika called. "Ganga is here," she said, playing on the word *ganja*, which she did not want to say on the phone. Her parents would be out to a wedding that evening so I could come over. When I reached her house, her younger brother Avi opened the door. He studied at St Xavier's college in Bombay and was home for the summer. He gave me a sour smile. Ruchika standing behind him mouthed "He knows." As we walked toward the living room, I tried to ease him into our adventure, asking him if he had tried weed. He growled an emphatic no, as if offended by the question. On further goading, he admitted that he had seen his friends at college use it, quickly adding that he did not approve of it, his tone bristling with self-righteousness.

"Aren't you a little too serious for your age?" I joked. "You know, I had an uncle who quoted Marx like nursery rhymes when he was in college and was eager to change the world. You know what he is doing today? Working for a multinational."

Avi stared at me. "So?"

"What is the moral of the story?"

He shrugged.

"Don't take yourself too seriously. Life will find a way to laugh at you."

"Hmm—I wonder why people feel compelled to dispense unsolicited wisdom," Avi said with disdain and left the room.

"Acid tongue runs in the family," I mumbled.

"Well, we-don't-suffer-fools runs in the family," Ruchika said with a chuckle and handed me a small zip-lock pouch the size of a pan-masala packet.

I ignored her barb and opened the tight wad. Its content was not in the form of the crushed dry leaves I had seen and expected. The material was a dark lump of paste, the texture and feel of Play-Doh. I smelt it. It was good old dope all right.

"I have no idea how to use this putty."

"Don't tell me you are as useless as I've always suspected you to be," Ruchika retorted.

I asked her to bring me a white sheet of paper. Placing it on the glass top of the coffee table, I crumbled the substance into tiny, sticky little lumps with my fingers. I loosened the tobacco from a cigarette on to the paper and mixed the weed particles—which now looked like rat droppings—into it. Then on a rolling paper I spread the mixture along its length. Ruchika kept watching me, and as I looked up, I could see an impish smile on her lips. By now she knew that I was a rookie, and perhaps more useless than she had thought. I persevered, not caring about my declining esteem in her eyes.

"How did you get hold of this," I said, trying to distract her attention from my fumbling.

"Seeing how inept you're, I'm not sure if it was worth it."

She never lets up, does she? I thought.

The rolled-up joint was loose and limp, as though it had endured the rigours of a sugarcane crusher. There was no way it was going to stand the test of fire.

"This will not work," I said in frustration. I emptied the joint and filled its content back into the hollow cigarette tube and tapped its filter on the glass top to pack it in snug.

"We're ready," I said, proud of my inventiveness.

Ruchika was unimpressed. We went to her bedroom window, which overlooked the street. "Don't open the window too wide," she said. "I have snoopy neighbours. If they even get a whiff of what we are up to, the heavens will fall."

"When did you start caring about others?"

"Oh God, you've no idea how they carry tales."

I lit the cigarette, and we took drags. We smoked the whole thing and waited. Nothing.

"Maybe you didn't use enough weed," she said.

"I don't know how to work with rat droppings."

"Oh, don't give me that. You can't work with *anything*. I can see that."

"That's a bit severe."

"You can't roll a bloody joint."

"Caveat emptor, my dear, caveat emptor," I said defiantly.

By this time, the house was stinking of dope. Avi came out of his room, sniffing. I asked if he had any idea how to make this Play-Doh work. He hesitated for a moment, then came and sat beside me. "I've only seen my friends do it," he said, taking over the production. The smell of weed, it seemed, had mellowed his moral fervour.

"Let me get something," he said. He came back with a safety pin. Using the sharp end, he picked a small lump of weed.

"For your information," he said, "this is hash, not weed. I thought you should at least know what you are consuming." Then, addressing his sister, "Don't for a moment assume I've done this before. I'm just repeating what I've seen my friends do."

Ruchika nodded and looked at me, trying hard not to laugh.

Avi held up a lump of hash on the pin, then put it to the flame from a cigarette lighter. It caught fire. But before it could burn out, he doused the flame, and with his forefinger and thumb, crushed out crumbs of dry powder onto the white paper. He repeated this till everything on the pin was reduced to crumbs.

"This is better than rat droppings," I said. "Thank you."

Avi left the room. I packed the material into another cigarette and we inhaled with trepidation, expecting our brains to go bananas with each drag.

"You feel anything?" Ruchika asked.

"A slight buzz," I said.

"I feel nothing," she said.

We tried another round and in a few minutes my head began to go soft. I could feel my brain lose its moorings and my body drifting in ether. In the next instant, the whole room was lifting up like a balloon. I was still conscious of my surroundings, though, alert to Ruchika sitting across from me. I could see time literally *moving* as though it were a physical object. I tried to keep pace with it, urging it to take me along. I started talking all sorts of nonsense.

"Hey Ruchika, I want to tell you something," I stammered, at one point. "This life you know that we live . . . somebody else is dreaming it up . . . now don't ask me who that . . . somebody is, okay? It just is . . . I can see it . . . I swear I can!" My speech was slurred and I had no control over the words stumbling out of my mouth.

"Looks like it has hit you," I heard Ruchika say.

"We're just puppets . . . and somebody is pulling our strings . . . bloody puppets, ha ha . . . goddamn puppets ha ha . . . !"

The room seemed to be floating upward at a gentle speed and also revolving as though on an axis. I was convinced that the puppeteer was having fun at our expense. I saw Ruchika laughing; her face appeared radiant and fetching. I felt a twinge.

"I've been meaning to tell you, Ruchika" I muttered, "You know I like you . . . like meaning . . . love you . . . like really love you . . . I bet you knew that . . . !"

"Gosh, this thing has hit you hard," I heard her say.

"You've no feelings for me, haan?" I closed my eyes and suddenly I was on a merry-go-round spinning fast. I was not sure how long I was in that state, but when I opened my eyes, the universe seemed to have stabilized. Ruchika was standing in front of me, the expression on her face a curious mixture of amusement and worry.

"Are you all right?" she asked.

"My throat is dry," I said.

"I'll get you some water."

"No, I don't think I can drink anything. My stomach is rebelling."

"Oh, no. I know what you need. Lime water with salt and sugar."

I sipped the concoction but knew I would not be able to keep it down. I was trying to remember what I was jabbering before but my attention was now grabbed by my gut, which seemed to be in full-blown revolt. I walked to the window, saying I needed fresh air. I started retching, and before long was vomiting out of the window, on to the overhang below and then the street. Disgusting. Good thing that it was past nine o' clock on a Sunday evening. The street was empty, the windows of the nosy neighbours tightly shut. There were no witnesses to my shame, except Ruchika. I wished she would leave me alone.

I stood at the window for a long time, and with each barf my innards wanted out. I felt drained and empty, and kept wiping my mouth on the handkerchief Ruchika had handed me.

"We should go up on the terrace. The fresh air will do you good," she said.

I followed her up, unable to speak. She offered me the lime water again. I sipped at it, and this time it felt good, and the fog in my brain seemed to be clearing. I stood reclining against the railing with a glass in one hand. I must have cut a tragic figure, a rakish film noir character with whom destiny had finally caught up. Instead of the altered state of consciousness I had hoped for, I experienced hallucinations and now was wracked by a gut-wrenching discomfort. I knew I was not going to die. Nobody dies of weed, I had heard it said. It was only a matter of time before my stomach settled. I looked up at the sky. It was dark and peppered with stars, like spilt salt, and the air was dry. We stood there like shadows.

After a while, when I felt that I could hold it down, Ruchika offered to drop me home. In the car she kept looking over at me. "You've no stomach for fun," she said. "Look, what a weak-hearted, lily-livered guy you are!"

She was her usual self again. Her taunt, her cackle helped lift the haze.

"The stuff rattled me up all right!" I chuckled. "But you rode it quite well it seems."

"Just a zing, but no barfing, no blabbering."

"Sure, rub it in, I expect nothing less from you." After a pause, I asked, "So what was I blabbering about?"

"You were spilling the secrets of your heart."

"Oh God, no! What was I saying."

"That you love me."

I was quiet for a moment. It was just as well, and I thought perhaps it was a good opportunity to fess up to it.

"That is true," I said softly and looked at her.

Her eyes were on the road, her face impassive. Presently, she was distracted by a scooter that cut in front of us. "Idiot," she cursed.

Soon we left the cacophony of the traffic behind us as we entered the residential area. Houses on both sides of the street showed no signs of life but for the television screens flickering through some of the windows. Ruchika pulled up at our front gate. I kept sitting, waiting for her response.

"You want me to open the door for you, sir?" she said in a mocking tone.

I shook my head in frustration and got out and did not bother to thank her. How could she be so insensitive, I thought. She waited in the car and watched me till I reached the building gate. When I turned, she waved a goodbye.

I made an effort to steady my steps, and made it to our flat hoping not to disturb anyone. My parents seemed to be asleep, but the lights were on in my sister Meeta's room. I padded to my own room and crept into bed. Propping up my back with pillows, I lay down in a half-reclining position. Ruchika's silence continued to trouble me; I felt humiliated and chided myself for being a fool. I waited for sleep to come.

Instead, I sensed a sudden dull rumbling in my chest, and my heart gradually picked up speed. Soon it was throbbing like it had fallen in love. I panicked, gasped for breath. What was it now? Was it the shame of being spurned or weed taking its toll? Maybe Ruchika was right, I was weak-hearted, after all. As I panicked over my condition, Meeta walked into my room.

"Where have you been this late?" she inquired.

I pressed my chest with my hands to keep it from pounding. Noticing my discomfort, she walked up to the bed and checked my forehead. I told her what I had been up to and that my chest was going wild as a result. She gave me a long despairing look and then went to the kitchen and came back with a glass of water and a Panadol.

"Take this," she said and started calling the doctor.

Summer nights are quiet in Udaipur. After ten, the city is dead to the world. By the time we found ourselves outside the doctor's house, waiting for someone to open the door, it was almost eleven-thirty. Our very presence out there at that late hour seemed to be a violation against the calmness that lay over the city like a warm blanket. Even the dogs had the good sense not to bark.

The doctor's son opened the door and greeted us, stifling a yawn. We found the doctor at his desk in his bedroom. A stethoscope dangled from his ears. He motioned me to sit in a chair next to him.

"Sorry to bother you at this hour, doctor sahab," Meeta said.

"Not at all," he said, somewhat wearily. Then, giving me the look of a man who had spent a lifetime being rudely woken up at odd hours of the night, he asked, "What happened?"

I explained without mentioning the weed. He examined my chest and back with the stethoscope and checked my blood pressure.

"Everything looks normal," he said. "But I want you to get an ECG done right away."

"Now, at this hour?" Meeta asked.

"Yes, I don't want to take any chances. All the labs are now closed of course, so you'd better go to the general hospital. Once you get the report, please call me."

I mumbled a thank you, and Meeta once again apologized for bothering him at the late hour.

As we walked home, which was not very far, we debated what to do.

"An ECG is not necessary. We know why this ticker is excited," I volunteered.

"Maybe, but we must get it done. Let's go to the hospital," said Meeta.

"We won't get an autorickshaw at this time," I said in an attempt to dissuade her. But she had made up her mind. When we reached the end of the street, there was no autorickshaw in sight. "Let's go to the main intersection," Meeta said. "Hopefully we'll find an auto there."

We walked in silence. My chest still hurt, but the heart was still uneasy over Ruchika's cryptic silence. If she had feelings for me she would have confessed. Disappointment like a concrete ballast began to sink in my stomach. We reached the intersection where a tea stall was still open. A few late-nighters huddled around, chatting and sipping tea. There was an auto a few paces away, but it was occupied. Meeta approached the driver, anyway. On learning that we wanted to go to the hospital, the driver and passengers agreed that if anyone on the planet needed the auto most, it was us. The passengers—two village women with small children—got out and said that they would wait for the driver to return. Why they were waiting there in the middle of the night, one would never know. The driver quoted a price and Meeta readily agreed.

"You don't want me to drive fast, do you?" the driver asked, looking over at us.

"Not too fast," Meeta said.

The driver must have been in his forties. Dark as coal, the whites of his eyes looked as though floating. His khaki overalls were long overdue for a wash.

"The moment I heard 'hospital,' I had to come," he said. "Couldn't let you die."

I skipped a heartbeat when he said that. Do I look that bad, I wondered. Meeta thanked him for his kindness, and on reaching the hospital, gave him two 100-rupee notes. He looked pleased.

I had imagined the emergency unit as a place with patients lying on the floor, and medicine bottles and bits of bandage strewn all over, but it turned out to be surprisingly clean and spare. There was hardly anyone around, other than a couple of policemen sitting by the door, killing time. The clerk at the front desk noted down my details and directed me to the doctor's room. There were three men there, sitting around a refectory table, drinking tea.

Which of them was the doctor, I wondered. They were all

young, in their early thirties. Dressed in a slovenly manner, they gave the impression that they had strayed in from the street to unwind after a hard day's work, and not had the time to shower. They glanced at us, then continued with their banter.

I hesitantly approached the one who had a stethoscope around his neck, and handed him the form. He looked at it and asked me a few questions about my condition.

"Aah, you had cheese, no wonder you vomited. Never eat cheese from the bazar," he said, and asked me to go to the ECG room. "Out straight and turn left."

In the ECG room, two young men had their heads buried in smutty magazines. From their appearance, it seemed that they too had wandered in from the street. I noticed the bed where I was to lie down for the examination. The sheet and pillow cover had not been changed in at least a hundred years. Sweat and soil from a million people had accumulated on them in layers of black grime. Meeta and I looked at each other.

"Here? No way," I mumbled.

Before I could act on my impulse to make for the door, the man in charge took the form from me and asked me to lie down.

Sheepishly, I obeyed, summoning a strong inner resolve to levitate. Thankfully, the fellow was quick and helpful. In less than five minutes, I was up on my feet. On being asked, he said that the report seemed normal. The doctor confirmed it and gave me a prescription in case the chest pain persisted.

"You must fumigate your clothes and take a hot shower before you touch *anything* at home," Meeta issued the fatwa as we walked out, looking once again for an auto to take us home. It was way past midnight. We looked like refugees who had stumbled onto a lonely dystopian planet where all life had been destroyed. We walked past Chetak Circle, to the road across the roundabout leading toward Fatehpura. Four men were bent over an auto whose rear seat was upturned.

"Can't you see we are repairing the damn thing?" was the answer to my enquiry.

As we stood there contemplating our fate, a car sped by and screeched to a halt a few metres ahead. The driver asked where we were heading, Meeta explained, and we got into the car without any concern for safety. The question why this man was offering us a ride in the dead of the night didn't even cross my mind. He said he thought our auto had broken down and had figured that we needed a ride. He turned out be a private taxi driver.

"You're a kind man," I told him. On reaching home, I handed him some money. He refused. I insisted. He took it and thanked me, as if I was doing him a favour.

Ruchika called the following morning. "How are you feeling, my Romeo?" There was a hint of derision in her voice.

"God! Ruchika, can you ever be serious?" I said. I felt hurt. I had not slept well and was feeling sad and miserable and in no mood for her ribbing.

"Short answer is, No. Long answer, I like you, too, but not in the way you think. And it has nothing to do with you, personally. You're my good friend, close and pally and all, but . . . "

There was a pause, and I dreaded she would reveal another love interest.

" . . . but I'm not into men."

Not into men! The words rattled in my mind. The possibilities enunciated by those words were both thrilling and unsettling. Gender binary was all I knew and understood, but trust Ruchika to have demolished even that truth. It was a relief to know that there wasn't another man, but there was also a regret that she was beyond me in ways I had never imagined.

Woman of Substance

I had returned home to India after seventeen years and had been making the rounds, meeting relatives and visiting old haunts with childhood friends. One late morning I decided to pay a visit to our neighbour Asma Auntie. I went unannounced, as was normal here. To announce one's visit beforehand was to invite ridicule and the charge of snobbery. And knowing Asma Auntie, she would have mocked me no end. I knocked on her door twice, but then remembered Mother saying that she was hard of hearing and her room was at the back of the house. I entered and walked across the courtyard to where her room was. She was sitting in a chair looking out the window, which opened on to a quiet backstreet. A housemaid was making chapattis in a small kitchen attached to the room. The aroma of fresh baked dough filled the air and I felt a sudden pang of hunger.

I greeted Auntie. She merely nodded, failing to recognize me.

"I'm Arif," I said.

"What?" she said and fumbled with her hearing device. "I can't hear anything, something is wrong with this stupid thing. Can you check?" Her voice was loud.

The housemaid shook her head at me. "This is her daily thing. I keep shouting and all she does is nod. It's one-way street with her."

I took the ear-piece from Asma Auntie and examined it, fiddled with the settings and gave it back to her, "Okay, let's try now."

"Oh beta, it worked, you are a magician."

"Asma Auntie, you know who I am?"

She looked at me sharply through her thick glasses, her expression curious and searching. Her thin white hair was sparse and wispy. She had put on weight and her bulbous nose which had been pockmarked since birth sat grotesquely between her sagging jowls.

"Take a guess, Auntie, take a guess."

She stared with renewed intensity, and I saw her eyes light up.

"Arif? Is that you? Big man, haan! Oh, how's your mother? Haven't seen her in ages. Ask her why she doesn't visit me anymore. Oh, rascal, I still can't believe, it's you. You were such a tyrant, you remember? How you harassed my little Tasneem. Allah, what a devil's work you were! Now look at you, you look like a proper gentleman. Hope you also behave like one. Can't believe it! Whatever happened, who changed you? It has to be a woman. Are you married? Yes of course, you are. Couldn't you come and marry in here in your native town? And why such a rush, was the bride running away? Or was she pregnant? You never know these days."

Asma Auntie chuckled. "Don't mind me, okay, you know my tongue moves faster than my manners. Your mother showed me the photos. She's so pretty, your wife. What's her name, I forget. I'm sure she has put some sense into you, otherwise you were good for nothing. You know we women have that power. Look at you, my my, may Allah keep you safe and happy."

Asma Auntie paused to catch a breath and then yelled at the housemaid, "Shantabai, clean up properly, you always skip the corners. I know your kind, don't think you can fool an old woman." She then turned to me and seeing that I was still standing, reprimanded, "You need an invitation to sit?" I took the side of the bed beside her. She looked at me as though still not convinced it was me. A smile played on her lips.

"Tell me when did you come?" she asked. "I know you people only pay us flying visits, and off you go rush, rush, as if this place is studded with thorns. You know this town, this country is your home, this is where you grew up, your roots are here. No matter where you go, the pull of the homeland will bring you back. Tell me, are you happy there? Canada, right? Allah, what a godforsaken land you have gone to. I hear it is so cold there that even as you speak your words freeze. I can never understand why anyone would want to live in such a place. But you must be happy there. Bless you. And listen, you may think you're a big foreigner, but to me you are still that naughty, snotty Arif, and don't think I've forgotten all the heartache you caused my little darling."

The little darling was her daughter Tasneem with whom I played as a boy and often drove her to tears, teasing her, calling her fatso. She now lived in Dubai with her chartered accountant husband and two sons. Asma Auntie's son, Tauqir, who was older than me lived in Houston. A software engineer married to a white woman. They had a daughter. The photos of the two families in picture frames stared at me from the bedside table. Tasneem had lost her baby fat and looked slim and attractive. She was smiling, teeth showing. Her hands rested on the shoulders of her two sons, and the husband with a rotund belly was by her side, one hand in a pocket, looking grim. Tauqir looked older than his years, having garnered more fat overall and losing some hair. His wife sat in a chair, looking thin and sickly. Tauqir carried his baby daughter in his arms.

Asma Auntie nattered on, not allowing me a word edgeways.

"May I," I said wanting to answer the questions she was lobbing at me.

"No, you may not," she snapped. "I'm not done yet. You show up after ages and you are still so shameless as to interrupt me with your snooty 'May I.'"

I glanced at Shantabai half-amused, and she beamed her buck-toothed smile, shaking her head.

"Okay, now tell me what will you have? With all my talk I clean forgot to offer you anything. Shantabai, make him some tea."

"No Auntie, it's fine, I just had it at home."

"Shut up. Shantabai makes good tea. Here, I've something in the fridge that you will like." Asma Auntie raised herself with an effort and as I tried to lend her a hand she brushed me off. "I can manage very well, thank you." She waddled over to the fridge and brought a small bowl of China grass custard. Made of milk and flavoured gelatin, its pink translucent surface glistened like marble. I had never liked the stuff and was in no mood to eat it, knowing how impossibly sweet it would be. Eat, she commanded, handing me the bowl and asking Shantabai to get me a spoon.

I sat there with the bowl and the spoon in my hands and watched Asma Auntie as she resumed her seat. None of her feistiness had faded. Her husband had left her for another woman when the children were still small and she had brought them up on her own as a seamstress, catering for small gatherings and doing other sundry jobs. Mother had offered to help but Asma Auntie would not take money from anyone. On a shoestring income she had managed to give her children a good education and they were now leading successful lives with their families. Asma Auntie had done well by herself but seemed terribly lonely. Her failing ears only amplified her loneliness. She was a pragmatic, tough-minded woman and I doubted she ever entertained any notion of self-pity, or even of pride for having struggled alone.

"Are you going to sit there like a statue or eat that thing?" she said, irritated. "You foreigners make so much fuss about everything. What is it with you people? You won't drink our water, you think ten times before touching our food. You think our India is not good enough for you anymore, haan?"

I thought the best way to respond was to start eating. I reluctantly took a spoonful and was pleasantly surprised by its creamy, rich taste. "This is really good, Auntie," I said.

"Good, now better finish it."

I cast my eyes around the room. I had been here last when I was a gangly teenager, and I could see that time had not been kind to the place.

"Looks like everything is falling apart, right?" she said with a smile. "When Tasneem comes, she's always nagging me 'why don't you get new furniture, why don't you get a new paint, why don't you upgrade the bathroom, why don't you do this, why don't you do that . . . ' but beta, I'm old and how many more years do you think I have left?" Her tone became grave and she sank back in her chair with a sigh. "I pray to Allah daily, take me while I'm still on my two feet."

"Auntie you'll live long . . . "

"Don't give me your false comfort, beta," she cut me off. "I've lived long enough, and I won't say it has been easy, but life is like a game of cards, you make do with the hand you get. But I must say your mother was very kind to me. I'll always be grateful to her. But unfortunately," she suddenly perked up, "I cannot say the same thing about you, you rascal." She smiled playfully revealing her missing teeth. Her nosestud emitted a dull gleam.

"Auntie, may I ask you something?"

"Only if it's not something stupid."

"Why didn't you marry again?"

"I knew it, you are incapable of intelligent thought," she said and rapped me on my knee. "You think I'd burn myself twice! You think I'd trust a man again!"

I felt foolish and looked away at Shantabai who had started making tea. I instructed her to use very little milk and no sugar, but she didn't pay heed: apparently a milk-laden, sweet tea is what a visitor and a foreigner deserved. I sipped the brew with great reluctance and tried to finish it, fearing Asma Auntie's censure. When it was time to leave, I pressed a five-hundred rupee note in her hands as I kissed them. On feeling the paper she recoiled as though from a current. "No, no I cannot accept this," she said. I insisted. "Rascal, look what a gentleman you've become!" Then turning to Shantabai, she intoned "You can't imagine what a horror show he used to be." I smiled sheepishly. Shantabai had finished cleaning up. I paused at the kitchen door and quietly handed her a couple of notes. She hesitated for a moment then clutched them deftly in her fist.

Friend and Philosopher

On the plane as I flew back to Toronto I fondly recalled my visit to Asma Auntie. Her words "horror show" kept buzzing in my mind. Was I that bad? Those early years now seemed so distant as though it were another life in another age. And of all things Asma Auntie remembered only my mischievousness. Surely, there was more to my childhood than that but she saw me only as the tormentor of her daughter. And that was that.

As I sat back sipping tomato juice, the drone of jet engines humming in the background, I pondered over the capriciousness of our memories. It seems they are nothing more than the feelings that refuse to die. Asma Auntie's long forgotten emotions got triggered on seeing me. But she was not far off the mark. No wonder she had a hard time accepting that I was the same raffish boy of all those years ago. She would have fallen off her chair with thigh-slapping mirth if I had told her that I had become a life-coach and a mentor who helped people improve their lives.

Even for me, when I think about it, the transformation has been quite dramatic. Asma Auntie had hinted that my wife may have had a hand in my metamorphosis but that was only partly true. Smita did help smoothen the rough edges of my personality and hone my social skills, but the real impetus for change had come from Rahul.

Rahul was like an avatar who came into my life out of nowhere and then disappeared all too soon. His father, a school principal, had been transferred from Lucknow to a government-run school in our town. Rahul, though, joined the private convent school to which I went. He was different, the way a cheetah is different from a hyena. It was not a difference of degrees but of species. The graph of his evolution was off the charts, or so it seemed. Being a Lakhnavi he spoke Urdu in an accent and with a vocabulary I had never heard anyone speak. And he was Hindu. This contradiction alone was enough to shatter the smug underpinning of an ignorant oaf like me.

There was something about him, in his manners, in his speech, in his actions that gave off an air of sophistication. I don't think he was even aware, at least initially, of the effect he had on me, and perhaps on many others. In hindsight, I can assess and delineate his many qualities that I had come to admire. But at that time I did not have the acumen for such analysis. He was just different, and I wanted to be like him. He had an angular face, a sharp nose, serious eyes and a shock of wavy black hair covering an elongated head that glowed, to me at least, with intelligence. He didn't strike one as handsome, but he effected a certain suave, effeminate charm like a nawab. Boys began calling him that.

Rahul had joined us in Class 9 in the middle of the school year, and on the first day when the teacher introduced him, he came up to the front of the class and recited a poem in English. He said he had written it for us, his classmates. I was impressed.

Later that morning during the lunch recess I sought him out and made his acquaintance. We discovered that we lived in the same neighbourhood and that helped matters along. I asked him about his hobbies. Reading books and writing poems, he said.

I stared at him in wonder. He said he read Enid Blyton and the Hardy Boys, names that had never touched my ears. They were English story books, he added by way of explanation. Then he said he also read story books in Hindi and Urdu. He knows how to read Urdu, I thought, flabbergasted. His repertoire included Ibne Insha, Premchand, Ismat Chughtai, Harivanshrai Bachchan and many others whose names were strange and alien to me.

He wanted to read Ghalib and Meer also, he said, but they were not easy to understand. His father had told him to wait a few more years. One may understand the meaning of individual words, he said, but their cumulative meaning comes to those who had lived life. "Father says that the secret to what writers say is held by life, and only age and experience can unlock that secret."

I nodded as if I understood exactly what he meant. Here was a guy talking about books and writers I had never heard of, and of ideas that bounced off my head. And there was I, a moron who took pride in *not* taking anything seriously. For the first time in my life I felt a sense of inferiority. With just a few minutes of his talk Rahul instilled in me a feeling of dissatisfaction with myself. My first impulse was one of resentment: he was a pretentious nawabi dandy, showing off his superior upbringing to the likes of me, a crude and backward bumpkin.

We shared the desk in class and the following day he was a little late, and when he poked his head into the door the class had settled and the teacher had finished taking the roll call. He excused himself, saying he was sorry for being late and walked up to the desk with easy, natural confidence. Sixty pairs of eyes followed him. He gave me a shy, conspiratorial smile and sat down beside me. The first thing he did was open his bag and hand me a bunch of Hardy Boys books. You will enjoy these, he whispered.

Later that evening after school I did not go out to play. After washing up and eating a snack, I took the books out of my backpack. There were five slim volumes as good as new with colourful covers emblazoned with ominous titles. I had never read a novel before and felt overwhelmed. Will I be able to read even one of these? I picked the title that seemed most exciting, *The Secret of the Caves* and dove right into it.

Mother was busy in the kitchen and Father and Brother were out. Soon my friends came calling, and Mother, not expecting me to be home, told them I was out already. After a while they came back reporting I could not be found anywhere. Mother told them to look harder, for she could have bet anything that if I could be found anywhere in the world after school it would not be at home.

Reading a book was a novel experience for me. It was hard going through the first few pages and there were many words new to me whose meaning I did not understand. I guessed their meaning by context but realized this was no way to enjoy a story. I complained to Rahul the next day and he advised me that I should look up a dictionary. He himself did not understand a lot of words and always kept a dictionary handy.

"Do you have a dictionary?"

I stared blankly, thinking why in the world would anyone need a dictionary?

"You better buy one. The Oxford English Dictionary is the best," he suggested.

That evening at dinner I expressed my desire to buy a dictionary. Everyone froze. Mother in the act of scooping rice, Father as he was breaking a piece of chapatti and my brother Irfan with his morsel midway to his mouth. They looked at me as if I had uttered a heresy.

"What?" I said, fully aware why my words had caused such paralysis.

"Say that again," Irfan demanded, "what did you just mumble. I'm not sure I heard you right."

I repeated. Mother and Father smiled and exchanged a look. Their wayward son had at last seen the light. Irfan, however, was not that charitable.

"Do you even know what a dictionary is?" he quipped. "It is not a book of tricks, you know?"

"I know what it is, bhai," I said ignoring his sarcasm.

"And why do you need it? You wanting a dictionary is like a thief wanting to be a priest."

"Now stop it!" Mother scolded him.

I was expecting the ridicule and was determined not to allow Irfan to get under my skin. I said calmly that I had started reading story books and wanted a dictionary to know the meanings of words.

"You reading for pleasure? Can someone please call a doctor!"

"Shut up, Irfan," Father said. "If he wants to read, shouldn't you encourage him instead of harassing him." Father smiled and then his smile broke into a wild sputter. Everyone joined in. What a supportive family I had. My desire to better myself had turned into a joke. Blood rushed to my head, it felt heavy with insult and injury. I got up in a temper and stormed out. Mother called after me to finish my food.

I went down to the front door and stood there fuming. I wished Rahul were my brother. Why was I not born in his family? Two houses down across the street, Asma Auntie's daughter Tasneem and her friend were chatting. I could hear the murmur of their voices. I wanted to call out to her, Aey Fatso! to vent my anger but stopped. Presently I heard footsteps behind me and felt a slap on my back.

"What are you sulking for?" Irfan scolded. "Okay, listen, I'll buy you a dictionary, now stop moping like a girl. It doesn't suit you."

"Go away," I said. "I don't want your frigging charity."

He slapped the back of my head lightly. I pushed him away. He lunged at me. I grabbed his shirt collar and tried to headbutt him in the chest, but he being taller and stronger wrapped his hands around me and pulled me toward him. Hugging me and shaking me from side to side like a sack of potatoes, he cooed, "Oh, my little scholar is angry. Daddy is going to buy you a new toy, okay raja?" I gave him a violent shove and stomped away.

The following day after school I found a package wrapped in brown paper tied with a white string on my desk. For the next few days I consulted the dictionary furiously, exulting in the revelation after revelation it threw up at me. School, homework and reading became an endless loop, and there were times when I was in bed with a book late into the night. Irfan, with whom I shared the room, would badger me to go to sleep.

My playmates came calling and went away disappointed. They could not understand how a person who was normal till yesterday could change so suddenly. I told them about my new-found love for books and they said the devil had definitely taken hold of me. I saw pity in their eyes. You know where to find us were their parting words.

As I immersed myself in the mysteries of the Hardy Boys, I was enraptured by their strange and enticing universe; the lives of the characters, their schools, their friends, the things they were up to were so foreign and exciting; the way they talked and the mysteries they solved and the intelligence they possessed made me feel small and I became acutely conscious of my inadequacies, my joyless life and my insignificant and limited small-town existence.

On top of that, Rahul had put me in an intellectual funk; his presence had created a cerebral vacuum that my whole being was driven to fill in the shortest possible time. I had so much catching up to do. After weeks of intense reading, during which I had shut out play completely, at Mother's insistence I occasionally started going out with friends. And although it was good to be out again in the rough and tumble of play, I realized that a certain sobriety had crept up inside me. I was forever lost in the rarefied narratives of fictional characters and their impossible lives. I stopped harassing Tasneem and it seemed she felt neglected and ignored. In school my grades improved, and at home my reputation. Father gave up his vigil over my studies, and Mother was mostly indulgent but worried that I was spending too much time with books. Go out and play a little, she would say. I never imagined I would hear those words from her.

In school Rahul and I spent most of our time together and I visited him at his home most Sunday afternoons. We talked about books, of course, and movies and cricket and other random things. And girls. Yes, girls. Rahul had a crush on Malavika, the pretty, doe-eyed damsel who lived on his street. But Malavika seemed not to care about him. Rahul asked me for tips on how to get into her good books. Get her interested in books, start from there, I advised. The next thing I knew, he lent her a *Romeo and Juliet*. That did not go down well, apparently.

Rahul's family was virtuous and high-minded, as though pegged to an unattainable ideal. His mother, a sweet woman, was always smiling, and his father, a little heavy-set, was gentle and genial—so unlike a principal. They addressed each other with respectful pronouns and employed the royal "we" for themselves. I felt out place in their home and, in the initial days, tried to be on my best behaviour. But to their credit they never made me feel different. As time passed, I not only shed my inhibitions but also came to know Rahul better. His intelligence and literary prowess were beyond reproach, no doubt, but I discovered that he was not the paragon of perfection I had made him out to be.

I had asked him to teach me Urdu, and he had happily obliged. But it soon transpired that he was not a good teacher. He had little patience with my slow progress as I struggled to decipher the words and would often get angry over my sloppy handwriting. I would protest that the Urdu script was alien to me, and my hand was not used to moving from right to left while at the same time staying true to the twists and curls of the letters. He would dismiss my genuine grievance as laziness.

I also detected a touch of arrogance in him, especially when he recited poem after poem from memory. The feat was impressive indeed, and one could be persuaded to concede him his cockiness. But I couldn't be. I was jealous, perhaps. On one occasion I made so bold as to tell him he was a show-off. He was unperturbed and said if one possessed talent then there was no harm in flaunting it. I said I would like to flaunt my karate kick, and he burst out laughing. He slowly warmed up to my carefree nature and my crude, irreverent jokes. I would often tease him about his clipped speech and exaggerated Lakhnavi courtesies. And he would call me a peasant and make fun of my lack of etiquette. We began to laugh at each other, and laughter saved us. It broke barriers and egos. The aura that I had conjured around him began to fade. We became friends.

But I continued to consider him my guide and philosopher, and looked to him for inspiration. Almost a year had passed since I opened that first book that I read. In that time I had devoured a lot of light adventure stories but eventually grew weary of their shallow, predictable plotlines. Rahul advised that it was time to graduate to the classics, to Manto and Dinkar and Dickens and Twain and Defoe.

I distinctly remember the day I brought Defoe's *Robinson Crusoe* home from the library. It was a Sunday morning, a bright autumn day, the sun was making its steady climb across a clear blue sky. The rays fell on me warmly as I sat in a corner on the terrace. I had doubled up a mattress to sit on and propped my back against two pillows. I stretched out my legs, looked around to make sure nobody would disturb me. The hardbound volume with its white glossy cover felt smooth to the touch. I caressed it as if it were a pet. It appeared to be a new virgin copy which nobody had yet opened. I brought the book close to my nose and smelled it. It smelt of happiness, or so I thought. The feeling was close to what could be termed as ecstasy. I opened the novel gently. I lapped up the words until noon, by which time the sun was in the zenith and its scorching heat, of which I had become unaware, would have surely singed me if Mother had not broken my spell by calling me for lunch. In a daze I climbed down the stairs flush with fiction and heat.

One Sunday afternoon at Rahul's place, we were sitting in the living room and chatting about something innocuous and the talk devolved into an argument and Rahul called me ignorant and dumb. His tone was serious, heavy with hauteur. I tried to laugh it off. His father, who was standing by the window, overheard the conversation and issued a reprimand to Rahul. He asked Rahul to go to him. Rahul got up and walked to his father with his head bent down. "How many stars are there in the universe?" his father asked. Rahul shook his head. "What is the size of an atom?" No response. "How many hairs on your head?" Rahul was mum, his eyes glued to the floor.

"What a duffer you are!" his father said in the voice of a principal. I had never seen him speak in such a stern register before, and knew instinctively that some sacred family tenet had been breached. He raised Rahul's chin with his hand. Rahul's eyes were welling up. "My dear boy," he said, "we're all ignorant of things in our own way, your little knowledge should not make you proud. Knowledge is one of those things that you increase by sharing."

Rahul stood still with his hands behind his back, his fingers fidgeting nervously.

"Have you heard of Rumi?" his father asked. Rahul nodded.

"Rumi said that when a candle lights other candles it loses none of its light." He reached again for Rahul's chin and asked him to look him in the eye. "Be that candle," he said and pulled Rahul toward his chest and patted his back.

Rahul shuffled back to where I was sitting. He said sorry softly. A tear trickled down his cheek.

Later that summer at the end of Class 11, Rahul would leave town, his father had been transferred to Bhopal. Rahul came over to my house to bid goodbye and we went up to the terrace and stood at the parapet looking out over the neighbourhood. The night was descending stealthily and lights were coming on in houses. An uneasy silence straddled between us. Normally Rahul was chatty but he too was quiet. A lump began to form in my throat as I pondered over my future which, without him, seemed bleak. After a long moment, Rahul turned to me and said, "Parting is such a sweet sorrow. Shakespeare's words those, and I used to puzzle over their meaning. Now I know."

I had no suitable response, literary or otherwise, and simply looked in the distance, gratified that Rahul was feeling the same way as I did. I wanted to tell him how he had changed my life but a mix of emotions deluged my heart and words failed me. It was getting close to supper time and Rahul said he should leave. We made our way downstairs; at the door he took my hand and pulled me into an embrace. Then he turned abruptly and left. I watched him go until I could see him no more.

Light as a Butterfly

A haze hung in the sky, as it always did. Gaurav couldn't remember when he had last seen the sky clear and blue. The sun pierced through the haze in a diffused white incandescence that stung his skin. Gaurav asked Bhima if it might rain.

The young boatman looked up, shielding his eyes with his hand. "Can't say, sir-ji," he said, speaking loudly to make himself heard over the sputtering of the outboard motor. "There was a time when we could smell rain in the air. The sky was our map, the wind our messenger. But of late, even the old-timers can't predict anything. Something has gone wrong."

Bhima was in his twenties, but his eyes were old and weary as though they had seen enough of the world already. His skin was dark, his hair tousled and unwashed. He stood with his feet apart, and his half-buttoned shirt flapped madly in the wind. The spring heat, even in the early hours, was already broiling him. The tiller vibrating like a piston beneath his hand, he guided the boat deftly through the calm waters.

He was chatty and eager to tell Gaurav about the vagaries of the weather, about life in the village, and its people, but when he was minding the motor, he appeared distant and cold. Gaurav found this behaviour strange. He listened as Bhima went on to explain the intricate cartography of the clouds that he had learned from his elders. The clouds that drifted in from the west were dark, but only for show, like the tusks of an elephant. Those from the east came laden with rain, filling wells and watering crops.

"What we fear the most are the ones from there," said Bhima, pointing toward the south. "They arrive suddenly out of nowhere and open up their fury. They flood our homes and fields, and when the water recedes, we count our dead."

Gaurav, born and bred in a city, had never before considered the movement of clouds or the significance of where they came from. His experience of the monsoon back home was to watch the skies turn slate grey and feel the cool breeze lift the heat. When it rained, children came out in the street and danced, open sewers choked up, and the traffic was a sodden mess.

Gaurav was a marine biologist in his early forties. He had an oval face, pudgy nose and rapidly receding hairline. His eyes were kind, his manner self-assured. Coming from a well-to-do family and having had the best education, he considered himself a cut above the average man. Studious and practical at the same time, he had come to believe that life was like a piece of wood that one could whittle into whatever shape one wanted. Work had brought him a long way from home, to rural Bihar. He was studying the effects of pollution on marine and riparian life, specifically at the Koshi River, which originated in the Himalayas and meandered down the plains before merging into the Ganga in southern Bihar.

That morning, he had arrived at the village riverbank in an auto rickshaw and enquired whether anyone would take him downstream. A number of fishermen had rushed toward him, pushing and shoving, offering their services. The river had run out of fish, so they were now reduced to fishing for tourists and visitors.

Despite being aware of their challenges, and though his project was about investigating the causes of the dwindling fish stock, Gaurav still found himself irritated at being accosted by a swarm of desperate boatmen. He ignored them and headed toward the river bank. The men followed him, pleading, even threatening. Gaurav had spied a lone boatman sitting by the shore, looking completely uninterested in soliciting his custom. Gaurav approached him and quickly agreed to his price without haggling.

His name was Bhima. He took Gaurav to the pier and helped him with his equipment.

Gaurav was a bit dismayed when he saw Bhima's boat. It was old and weatherbeaten, its red paint flaking. A few slats in the bed were also missing, exposing the metal base. "Are you sure this thing floats?" he asked.

Without bothering to answer, Bhima began loading the bags onto the boat. Gaurav stood on the sandy shore, not moving. "Come on, sir-ji," Bhima said then, "everything here is broken, but everything works."

Gaurav was not reassured. Reluctantly, he stepped on to the deck. He had both a fascination and fear of water. His dream was to own a house on the slope of a mountain from where he could see a lake and admire its beauty from afar. When he was near any body of water, he was nervous, for he could not swim. This was one of his abiding regrets.

Gaurav often wondered how a nonswimmer like him came to be a marine engineer. There was something incongruent about it, and the irony of it often made him smile. Today, as he climbed into Bhima's boat, that regret and fear resurfaced. He asked Bhima if he had a life jacket. Bhima shook his head. When Gaurav insisted on having one, Bhima went ashore to a fisherman's hut and borrowed a pair of floats—two metal tins, sealed and tied to the ends of a rope. Gaurav stacked them at his feet, within close reach.

"You can't swim?" asked Bhima.

"No," Gaurav said trying hard and failing to hide his embarrassment.

Bhima started the motor and the boat moved at a steady clip, the bow tearing through the muddy, placid waters. Gaurav grudgingly accepted the seaworthiness of the boat and relaxed, allowing the warm breeze to graze his face and lift his hair. A bright blue tarpaulin, precariously tied to four bamboo poles to provide shade, kept flapping in the wind. It looked like it would give way at any moment. Every ten minutes or so, he would dip a mason jar in the water, take a sample, then write on its lid with a black marker.

The river was wide at this stretch, its banks lined with trees and shrubs. Farther afield were farms lush with fresh crops, huts belonging to the farmers and fisherfolk dotting the landscape. There was something elemental and beautiful and tragic about the scene—nature's bounty and her unconditional generosity stood in stark contrast to the hard, austere lives of humans.

Gaurav had been watching Bhima and was struck by his air of arrogant, stoic indifference. The proud young captain commanding the stern, oblivious of his hand vibrating like a piece of machinery—as if it were not even a part of his body—his eyes unblinking, had taken no interest in what Gaurav was doing. Gaurav had tried to talk to him, but the noise of the motor had made it impossible.

After a couple of hours, Gaurav asked for a break. They stepped ashore at a tea shack. As they sat at the rickety, makeshift table, Gaurav asked, "Why didn't you approach me like other boatmen?"

"Oh, those men needed your money more than me. They have families to support."

"You don't have a family?"

"I have no one."

"What happened to your family?"

Bhima did not respond, stared at his hands. His nails were hard and overgrown, encrusted with dirt; the knuckles were knobby and rutted.

There was silence. Gaurav did not want to prod. He looked at the river, its gentle flow, the swirling eddies, the water lapping at the shore that was piled up with garbage and plastic. A young boy sat amidst the filth with a line cast, eating a guava.

"You know why I never learned swimming?" said Gaurav. "My father wouldn't let me go to the lake where the whole town came to bathe. He said the water was dirty. Once, when he was out of town, I went with my friends anyway. A friend pushed me in the lake saying that's how I'd learn. I almost drowned that day. I never went to the lake again."

Bhima smiled. "You come from a strange world."

"I guess. But I'm sure your father wouldn't have cared about the dirty water."

"I have no memory of living with my father or anyone else from my family," said Bhima. "All I remember is watching them die."

"Die?"

"Sometimes I wonder if it actually happened. I must have been five or six. Our small hut, not far from the banks of the Koshi, was swept away by the flood. My family had taken shelter in a tree. My baby sister slipped from my mother's hands. Mother jumped into the water after her, and then my father jumped in as well, trying to save them. The current was too strong. I never saw them again. I can still hear their cries."

Bhima spoke without emotion, without a sign of the pain such a memory might evoke. His eyes were hard, his voice flat. He seemed to be looking through Gaurav, not once meeting his eyes. Gaurav tried to imagine what it must have been like for him. It was obvious that this was not a story Bhima told often.

"The orphanage was in Patna, a big city," Bhima said. How he got there, he did not say. It was like a cage. The older boys were nasty; they had their gangs. You had to swear allegiance to someone—you couldn't be neutral. There were always fights and beatings. Even when they laughed, it was to mock someone. Every morning, classes were held to teach them Hindi and arithmetic. But the boys were too rowdy to focus on learning, and the teachers couldn't have cared less.

"Despite all that, I managed to learn to read and write. But I have not written anything more than my name. There were days when some of us were sent out to rich people's homes where middle-aged men played with us. For days afterwards, I would groan in pain.

"But the pain that terrified me the most was the memory of the flood which had taken my family. I would wake up screaming in the middle of the night and the boys would kick me for disturbing their sleep. The nightmare doesn't haunt me so often now, but once in a while, it rages through my sleep and I wake up shaking like a reed." Bhima paused and lowered his gaze.

Gaurav didn't know what to say. He wanted to know more but desisted from asking. He ordered onion pakoras from the tea shop, more for his companion than for himself, to fill up the uncertain silence. He normally didn't eat fried stuff from outside, but after hearing Bhima's story, his own dietary fastidiousness seemed frivolous.

Bhima didn't touch the fritters for a long time. Gaurav urged him to eat. He took a bite. "One day I escaped from that prison," he said. "There was this driver who had once come to pick me up for his master. I was about twelve or thirteen at the time, I think, and had no memory of my village. I told him about the big flood. He said my village must be along the Koshi River, because that was where the deluge had happened eight years ago.

"A few months later, the same driver came to pick me up again. On the way back, instead of taking me to the orphanage, he drove to the railway station. He shoved a few notes in my hands and told me to run away from that place—to take the train to Madhubani and find my way to the villages along the Koshi. I took his money and his advice. Since then, I've been wandering, looking for my village. Not that anyone is waiting for me there."

After a while they got up and started walking back toward the boat. "You own this boat?" Gaurav asked.

"Not in this lifetime!" said Bhima, laughing for the first time. "It belongs to some rich man. He himself lives in Darbhanga and has a manager in the village to look after his business."

"He pays you well?"

"He gives me fifty rupees a day on the days when I have a customer. No customer, no money."

"Only fifty rupees?"

"That's enough, sir-ji. If I have more, it gets stolen."

"You should open a bank account," Gaurav suggested.

Bhima gave him a look, perhaps wondering if he was being mocked.

"I'm serious." Gaurav said. "Put whatever little extra you have in the bank. In a few years, you'll have quite a bit. Then you marry, don't you want to? Get a wife, have children. You can start building a life, slowly. Then you won't be so alone."

Bhima stepped on to the boat, lowered the motor into the water and started pulling the starter. "And then one day there will be another flood. And all of it will be washed away," he said. The engine roared into life and a volley of exhaust smoke drifted toward Gaurav. He held his breath and waved his hand to clear the air. "Floods don't keep happening all the time," he shouted, but Bhima probably did not hear him. He was back at the stern, distant and aloof.

Gaurav thought about his own wife and daughter, his parents, his office, his friends and the myriad other people he had met and known. The bonds he had forged—some strong, some not so strong—together amounted to something—something that gave his life an anchor, a reason to wake up every morning, to work toward a goal, to provide for the family, to meet a friend and talk of old times, to dream of things, to have desires. He felt a mild resentment toward Bhima for being so cynical, for not wanting to improve his situation. Granted that he had had a hard life, that did not mean that all was lost and there was no hope. One couldn't go through life clinging to the past.

Gaurav, a practical man, believed in self-reliance. He lived by the dictum that nobody could help you if you did not want to help yourself. He had little patience with people who had no drive to make their situation better. He wished Bhima would snap out of his dark childhood—his smug victimhood—and realize that the world still had a lot to offer. Bhima was young and healthy. Gaurav had not seen him smoking. He had the potential to make something out of his life. Gaurav felt a sudden urge to mentor Bhima, to take him under his wing. So much youth and talent got wasted because many young people did not get the guidance they needed. He signalled Bhima to cut the engine. "Let the boat drift," he said, patting the space beside him to indicate that he wanted the young man to join him.

Bhima seated himself on the deck, outside the shade of the plastic tarp. A boat carrying hay and chopped wood passed them. Gaurav waved at the boatman. Taken by surprise, he grinned and shyly waved back.

"Where do you live?" Gaurav asked.

Bhima dipped his hand into the water, scooped a handful and hurled it in the air. A few drops splashed on them both. "In the village temple," Bhima said. "I pay a small rent to the priest, and he lets me sleep in a corner." He took another scoop of water and threw it heavenward. "I sleep in the shadow of the gods," he smiled.

Bhima said the priest, Purohit, was truly a man of God. Some people had objected to Bhima—a lower-caste person—being given shelter in the temple, but Purohit had told them to go take a dip in the Ganga. Purohit was fearless. He had left home a long time ago to seek moksha, and ended up in the village where Bhima lived. His extended family up north had a small business making soapstone figurines of gods and goddesses. Purohit, however, was drawn to the spirit of the deities, not their material form.

"Did he find it?" Gaurav asked.

"What?"

"Moksha, enlightenment."

"I don't know. I don't even know what that means. Purohit tried to explain to me, but my head is full of cow dung. He is a wise man, very knowledgeable. He gives me books to read, and I try to read them, but I can't focus on anything for more than ten minutes. My head begins to hurt."

Gaurav surveyed the river unrolling behind him like an endless ribbon, flanked by green, fertile earth. "This place is so beautiful," he said. "You must hate the river, though—it took away all you had," he added, even as Bhima looked around as if to reassess the familiar landscape in the light of Gaurav's comment.

Bhima did not speak for a while. He thumbed down a splint of wood sticking out from the plank. "No sir-ji, I don't hate the river. Koshi is our mother. She does not destroy her children. Look around, the beauty you are talking about is because of her. No, it is people like you—the educated folks—who come here and destroy everything."

"What do you mean?" asked Gaurav, taken aback.

Purohit had seen the changing fortunes along the river, said

Bhima. Not that everything had been fine and dandy in the past, but there had never been such catastrophes. The Koshi River brought rich silt from the Himalayas, a gift of the gods, and when she overflowed, she spread minerals on the plains, making the land fertile. Nobody had ever needed to use fertilizers and chemicals before. Life was hard but there was fish in the river, grain in the fields, and people were content.

"Purohit told me there used to be a natural rhythm to things—the seasons, the rains—the crops followed a pattern. It was like a dance, and men knew their steps. Now that music has stopped. Purohit said he has seen many tragedies but never before have tragedies been so bad as in the last ten or twenty years." Bhima paused, ripped off the splinter and chucked it in the water.

"And the disasters were brought on by men—educated men from Patna and Delhi—and by the bastard politicians. They started building dams on the river, as if she was their fathers' whore, as if they could do anything they pleased with her. These outsiders read a few books and think they can tell us what to do, how to live our lives. They have not grown a blade of grass in their entire lives and they lecture us on how to farm, what crops to grow."

"Purohit seems to have strong opinions."

"He is not wrong. He says floods are because of the dams. And because of them I lost my family."

The boat drifted with the current, losing direction; Bhima paddled with an oar to nudge it back on course. The sun was spitting fire. Gaurav urged Bhima to move into the shade of the awning.

Bhima managed an ironic smile. "What is left to burn, sir-ji?"

He eyed the paraphernalia Gaurav had brought along—vials arranged and labelled in a box, jars of water in a duffle bag, a microscope and other scientific instruments in another. Bhima picked up a vial and looked at it closely. "What is this for?" he asked. Gaurav detected sarcasm in his tone. He opened his mouth to answer, but Bhima had already averted his face and was looking away into the distance.

"What do you think it is for?" Gaurav asked.

Bhima shrugged and said he had seen many of his kind before. "They come and check the soil and sell us chemicals. They dump toxins in the river and kill the fish. They examine our cattle and give them injections. They come and build schools which have no teachers, clinics which have no doctors. They give us loans at high interest, and when floods destroy our crops and we can't pay back, they take our land, desperate farmers kill themselves." Every time he saw a city person, Bhima said, he knew trouble was not far behind.

"Yet without the city people, how will you progress?" Gaurav asked. "Purohit is telling you lies."

"Look at me, sir-ji. Am I a lie?" asked Bhima, looking Gaurav in the eye.

Gaurav was tongue-tied.

"Maybe Purohit is wrong," Bhima added. "Maybe I suffer only because of my sins."

"That's nonsense," snapped Gaurav.

"Purohit says the same thing. He says Brahmins have made up these stories to keep us down, to deprive us of knowledge, to keep us from progressing."

"For once that man is right. You should believe him on that," Gaurav said.

"I don't know, it is all too much for me, these complicated ideas. Purohit holds gatherings every Tuesday evening and many villagers come from far and near. He tells them that religion is not about bowing down before idols, it's about establishing Ram Raj, where everyone enjoys the bounties of mother earth equally. All the talk about sins and past lives is bullshit, he says. A few years ago, two fellows came to meet him and told him that he must continue with the good work he was doing, that people must be awakened. They said they were Naxalites from a neighbouring village."

"Oh, I know about *those* rebels," said Gaurav. "They think revolution will solve all our problems."

"All I know is that they support poor people," Bhima said.

"Why don't you join them, then? You have nothing to lose."

"I may lose my life," Bhima said sharply. "You know what happens to such rebels? They are killed like rats. One night a bunch of them hid themselves in the temple. In the morning, the police came and blew their brains out. The bloodstains are still there."

Gaurav winced.

"You know sir-ji, I take many people on this boat, and they lose no time telling me to do this and do that. I must look really miserable to you all," said Bhima, allowing himself a faint smile. "Purohit also used tell me not to waste my life. He would say, go serve people—there were many unfortunates like me. He told me to go to Patna and make a complaint against my old orphanage, rescue the boys who might be suffering. But I have no interest in all that." Bhima paused and paddled a few more strokes. "It's no use, sir-ji. We can't fight our fate. Purohit is wrong to give people hope."

Gaurav wished to counter his nihilism but checked himself. He absentmindedly dipped his hand in the water and was surprised at how cold it was.

"You should resume your work. We must turn back now," Bhima said, and before Gaurav could answer, he had risen, staggered to the back and started yanking at the engine, which came to life with a loud report. Once again, Gaurav stopped his breath and waved the fumes away from his face.

Bhima turned the boat around. Gaurav began taking samples and making notes in his diary. The sun had begun a slow descent from the zenith and was now catching Gaurav at an angle under the canopy, which still held, miraculously, despite fluttering fiercely in the breeze. The river was getting a little rough and there were waves slapping the sides of the boat. Gaurav looked for the floats and dragged them close to him with his foot.

His work suddenly seemed a little irrelevant to him. He had thought that science and technology had shepherded the human story on the path of progress. But now he was not so sure. For all his brash, cocksure approach to things, he hadn't been able to convey the value of his work to Bhima.

Purohit was not wrong. Not all men from the city came with good intentions. He himself had been asked to falsify reports, fudge data, and manipulate results. He had initially balked at such suggestions. But when faced with the choice between principles and a paycheque, he had picked the latter. He had not been able to afford the luxury of keeping a conscience *and* a livelihood. He wanted to tell Bhima that the work he was doing was deception, that he was a fraud, that everybody was out to line their pockets, that nobody gave a shit about the environment or the river or the people or their welfare. But Bhima knew that already; Purohit had educated him well.

He looked at Bhima, unwashed and uncouth, clothes dirty and ill-fitting, feet unshod and callused. Yet he was truly free—free of hope, ambition, and purpose, free of moral dilemmas, and light as a butterfly. A pang of envy pinched his heart.

The wind had begun to pick up and a sudden gust ripped the plastic awning. Bhima pointed at the clouds that were moving in, darkening the firmament. Clouds from that corner of the sky—the south—bring rain, not ordinary rain, but torrents. Bhima was smiling expectantly. Gaurav felt his stomach drop. The waves were becoming hostile, crashing and spilling over into the boat. The wind and water, it seemed, were in cahoots, their intentions not kind.

The boat began to sway, and Bhima cut the engine. Gaurav grabbed the floats and began to tie them around his chest. "What will we do now?" he asked, his voice laced with panic. There were no other boats in sight and they were far from the banks, so far that even Bhima would find it hard to swim back, Gaurav thought.

"Let us wait it out. That's the best thing to do. If I try anything, the boat might topple," Bhima said, almost shouting above the whoosh of the gale.

"Will this thing work?" Gaurav asked as he adjusted the floats. Bhima nodded. Gaurav, terrified, tightly clutched the plank he was sitting on. Bhima was still at the stern. He had upended the engine, and stood firmly, bracing for the storm, almost welcoming it. The boat began to drift toward the left bank, but it was still far.

Gaurav started praying, surprising himself that he had not forgotten, although he hadn't addressed God in a long time. The waves crested higher and higher and crashed down violently, almost tipping the boat over. Gaurav shouted. Was this the end? From the mood of the river, it felt like it was only a matter of time. A series of waves shook the boat, then came a surging heave that lifted the boat and overturned it. Gaurav saw Bhima diving. He wanted to shriek for help as he went down but lost his voice. The boat closed in over him. In a flash, he remembered the moment when his friend had shoved him into the water all those years ago. His head was submerged, he gasped and flapped his limbs. The floats kept him buoyant and as he raised his head, it hit the side of the boat. He grimaced in pain. He flayed his hands, trying to swim and get closer to the boat but it was sinking quickly. He turned toward the shore. The waves walloped him hard. His head was hurting but he was hardly aware of it. He desperately scanned the water for Bhima but he was nowhere to be seen.

He tried to swim. The bank looked far and was almost invisible, as it had now started raining. Sheets of water lashed down on his face. He felt alone—a strange, terror-filled, end-of-life aloneness. There was water everywhere, as if the universe itself had been churned into liquid. He spotted a figure swimming away, not very far. "Bhima, Bhima!" he shouted. "Here, here, please help." The figure kept moving away steadily, cutting through the water like a fish. Gaurav called out again and again, his voice hoarse and weak, but the figure did not look back. Perhaps he could not hear him.

Buffeted by the waves, lashed by the rain, Gaurav drifted downstream. It was getting dark. As he lost sight of the swimming figure, a shiver streaked through his body. He started beating his hands and feet furiously and tried to swim in the direction of the lone swimmer.